Spade

Fortuna Saga One

USA Today Bestselling Author
S.A. McClure

Be careful not to gamble away your soul.

Spade

Fortuna Saga One

USA Today Bestselling Author
S.A. McClure

Spade
Fortuna Saga One

Written by S.A. McClure

Edited by Leona Bushman

Cover Design by Jennifer Munswami of J.M. Rising Horse
Creations
https://www.facebook.com/groups/RysesCult/about/

Spade © copyright 2019. S.A. McClure

ISBN: 978-0-9992642-6-3

To my dear friend, Drew Bisson.

May you always remain lucky.

Chapter One

Amber flipped the death ace to the top of the deck. The hollow eyes of the skull printed in the middle of the spade stared up at her as she shuffled it back into the middle. Neon lights glowed above, casting a haze of color all around her. She yawned widely as she checked her watch. Ten minutes before the gamers started arriving. She still had ten minutes before she had to deliver that card to the unlucky player who'd gambled away his soul. He'd lost his bet, and now, Morta had come to collect.

Delivering the death cards to their victims was one of the many tasks Amber performed for her employer. She'd been assigned this role so many times, she'd nearly lost count. But, tonight's was different. Tonight, she was friends with the recipient. More than friends, really. At least, she thought they were.

The death card landed on top of the deck again. She trailed her fingers over the small scroll at the bottom. His name had been scrawled in a tight, cursive hand. It glimmered as it caught the light from one of the signs flashing above her. Her fingers trembled. She could tear the card up. Let the pieces drift away in the underground sewage pipes. Leave it all behind. Her stomach squirmed at the thought. Her place at Morta's side was all she needed. All she cared about.

"You look beautiful tonight, Fortuna."

Amber jolted as the sound of his voice pulled her from her thoughts. Her lips parted slightly as she gazed at him with hungry eyes. Her heart drummed in her chest. None of the guests were allowed to know her real name. They only knew her as 'Fortuna'—the goddess of luck. Her smiled faded as she met his familiar gaze. Acid swirled in her gut. Time was up. She swallowed, her jaw setting into a hard line.

"You shouldn't have come here tonight, Ethan," she whispered, her voice cold.

He sidled up to her, his eyes dancing with mischief. "Oh?" he asked as he leaned in to kiss her on her cheek. His smoky vanilla and cardamom scent sent a shiver of arousal down her spine. She slid her hands up his stomach until they were firmly pressed against his chest. His breath was hot against her skin. Goose bumps prickled the back of her neck as he growled softly.

She shoved him away before his lips met hers. The back of her throat felt raw and tasted of bile as she turned her face away from him. The attraction she felt for him wasn't worth it.

"Do you feel lucky tonight?" she asked as she took a step away from him. With space between them the mixture of heat and coiled anxiety in her stomach dissipated to a manageable level.

"With you around?" he countered. His hooded gaze roamed her body, lingering on the bodycon dress stretched tight across her chest. Amber felt the heat rise to her cheeks. He always had this effect on her.

She shuffled the deck. "Draw a card," she commanded.

His expression fell when he noticed the black, three-headed dog on the back of the cards. Everyone who was anyone knew what that design meant. Morta had made sure that the symbols of her gambling room, The Underground, were recognized by everyone in the 'V.'

"I just had one bad game," he said. "I swear I can pay it off. I just need a little time." He took a step back, his cheeks paling. "It was just one bad game," he repeated as if trying to convince himself.

Amber shrugged. No matter how much she liked him, he still owed a debt. Besides, it wasn't as if that was the first time she'd heard that excuse. From her experience, it was never just one bad night.

"You don't have to do this," he whispered, reaching a hand towards her. His fingertips barely grazed her cheeks as she turned her head away from him. She'd heard that one too.

"Just draw," she commanded, not meeting his gaze.

"I could leave," he said. His voice turned into a high-pitched fervor. "You could pretend I never came back here." He began shuffling backwards.

He was going to run. Amber knew he wouldn't get far. Knew that Morta would punish him if attempted it. She had a tendency to become vicious when crossed.

"It's too late," she called, jerking her head up toward the camera directly above them. Morta would already be on her way down to The Underworld's mouth.

"Please, Fortuna," he begged. Sweat gleamed on his brow as he ambled towards her. His eyes darted from side-to-side and his lower lip trembled.

How many times had she nipped at that lip during their time together? She closed her eyes and breathed in deeply before opening them once more to meet his gaze.

"I warned you," she whispered as she pressed the deck of cards into his hand. "Do you remember? That first time we met?"

She gripped his arm firmly. "I told you to be sure not to gamble away your soul." He attempted to yank his arm from her grasp.

She sighed.

Whether he drew the death card or not, Morta would collect what was due to her. Amber had never known her employer to forgive a debt of this nature. Sure, she had seen her erase entire columns of debt owed in terms of xandium—one of the rarest substances in the galaxy and the only known fuel source powerful enough to support the B-Drive—but never the energy she could steal from people. It just didn't happen.

"We could leave together," he pled. His eyes darted toward the door leading into the main gambling room. They were wrought iron with an intricate pattern of the ancient-Earth stories of Hades and his underworld. The tinkling of glass, whir of machines, and sound of laughter pulsed from just beyond them. They were revelries he would never experience again.

He cupped her cheek in his hand. "We could be together. It's what I've always wanted. You. Me. Far away from all of this." He swept his hand in the air, indicating the casino beyond them. "I have enough—"

His words were cut short as a tall, slender woman emerged from the entrance to the Underworld. Her silver-purple hair hung straight down her back. She wore a long black dress, which accentuated her curves. Her icy blue gaze locked onto Ethan as her thin lips curled into a smile.

Amber pressed the death card into Ethan's hand. It was the only response she could give him now. He shuddered at her touch. Her fingers curled into a fist. She understood his anger and sense of betrayal. Still, his reaction to her stung.

"We can work this out," he stammered. He attempted to step back, but Amber kept a firm grip on his arm.

Morta said nothing as she approached him. Amber looked away as liquid ran between Ethan's legs. She ignored the powerful scent of ammonia as it wafted past her.

"I can get the money for you. I just need more time," he murmured.

Amber hated it when Morta's guested begged when it was time to collect their debts. At times, it made her recoil away from the brutality of what her employer was about to do. Other times, it just made her loathe humanity even more. Of course, she had never been considered human. Not really, anyway. None of the naturally augmented humans were.

Morta wrapped her hands around Ethan's neck. He struggled against her. He thrashed. He moaned. And then, as Morta began pulling his lifeforce from him, he sagged. Her skin turned a glittering silver and his an ashen grey as his energy transferred to her.

When at last Morta removed her hands from around his neck, Ethan slumped to the ground. His face was gaunt, the skin stretched tight over his skull. He twitched slightly before stilling. No matter how times Amber saw what remained of the customers who gambled away their souls, she never got used to the husks left behind. Even his hair had turned into little more than a brittle, straw-like substance.

She swallowed the acid at the back of her throat and lifted her chin. There was no reason to look at him now. If he wasn't dead yet, he would be soon. She turned her attention to Morta, who still glowed from the transfusion.

"Walk with me," Morta commanded.

Amber slid the remaining cards into her dress pocket. Every single one of her dresses had pockets. It was one of the things she demanded from the seamstress she and Morta used for their evening gowns.

Morta linked her arm with Amber's as they strolled down Beauchamp Avenue. It was considered the main strip of the 'V' and housed all the best gambling houses the mining planet of

5

Thoth could contain. Morta owned nearly a third of the casinos in the 'V.' Her syndicate, known as the Underworld, was the second largest in the "V." Only the Taurus Syndicate was larger.

"I have a new job for you," Morta said.

Amber's heart beat rapidly, and she inhaled sharply. She was loyal to Morta. She would always be loyal to her above all others. At fifteen years old, she'd left Earth with nothing. Thoth had been the cheapest ticket she'd been able to get at the time, but she had been alone with no money on a strange planet.

Morta had taken her in.

Taught her how to better control her ability to manipulate quantum probability. Given her a family. All she asked for in return was the completion of certain tasks—like delivering the death cards.

"Oh?" Amber asked. No matter how strong her loyalty to the older woman was, she still hated new assignments.

Morta stopped walking in front of one of her many bars: Elysium. A massive tree—Amber knew it was fake—exploded from the roof of the structure. Everything was white and gold. Despite the dust in the air, this particular bar always seemed clean to Amber, almost sterile. Inside, she knew more plants, both real and fake, would create a garden-like ambiance. Morta had spared no expense to ensure that Elysium was a bright oasis in the dark twilight of Thoth.

"Listen to me, Fortuna," Morta ordered as she gripped Amber's shoulders tightly. "In the not so distant future, I intend to leave this empire to you." She tucked a stray lock of Amber's hair into a pin at the side of her head. Her fingered lingered on Amber's cheek. "I have had many protégés throughout the years, but none have shown as much promise, dedication, or loyalty as you."

Morta's icy-blue eyes roamed over Amber's face. Amber's stomach roiled at the thought. She had everything she could ever ask for. More than she had ever envisioned as a teenager still trapped within her uncle's clutches.

"You gave me a second chance," Amber whispered. "There's nothing I can do to repay you for your kindness all these years."

"Actually," Morta began, "there is."

Amber took a step backwards. "What do you mean? What can I do?"

Morta guided her into Elysium. She didn't say a word as she led Amber to the private room at the back of the bar. She held out her hand as a robot arm unfolded from the wall and pricked her finger with a needle. Morta grimaced, slightly before staring into the control pad's camera. The private room was only accessible through both retinal scan and blood diagnosis. It was here that Morta met with her naturally-augmented employees. It was also where she safeguarded her notes and plans for the Underworld.

Amber rubbed her pointer finger over her thumb's nail, lingering on the rough spot at its edge. Her palms were sweaty and she fought the urge to wipe them on her dress. The door pulsed as the bolts locking the door slid back, allowing them to enter. She half-expected to see Morta's entire squad of naturally augmented humans sitting around the conference table. She glanced side-ways at Morta as the motion-sensing light turned on.

The room was empty.

"What's going on?" she asked as she stepped into the room. The door slid shut behind her with a resounding thud. Her back stiffened. She clasped her hands behind, aggressively wiping the sweat from her hands onto the back of her dress.

Morta didn't respond to Amber's question as she strode across the room. She pressed one of the gilded panels. Soundlessly, it recessed into the wall and then a small door popped open.

Amber blinked. How had she never noticed the outline of the door before? She ambled across the room and trailed her fingers over the edges of the doorframe. Although they were smooth, she didn't understand how she had never noticed the outline before. She cocked an eyebrow at Morta.

Wordlessly, Morta slid past Amber and ducked beneath the low-hanging doorframe. Amber stared after her. Clearly, she was intended to follow, but the idea was wandering into the darkness below put a pit in her stomach. A cold breeze swept through the room, and the hair on the back of her neck stood on-end. Although her stabilizers didn't whir beneath her skin, she couldn't shake the tension rising from her stomach to her chest.

"Morta?" she called.

Her voice echoed down the hidden hallway. She stood on the precipice between the gilded room and the shadows. Her skin tingled the way it did when her body naturally began manipulating the odds in her favor. Usually, that meant her life was in danger, yet she couldn't imagine Morta ever doing something to harm her. Ignoring the tingling sensation, Amber stepped over the threshold and began following Morta down the hallway.

Chapter Two

Morta unlocked a series of doors which led deeper beneath ground. Each time they passed through a new doorway, the tingling sensation grew stronger. It was as if everything within Amber were screaming for her to run. To get out.

At last, Morta slipped a slender, black key from inside the folds of her dress. At its base, it had a skull shape with two rubies nestled into the eye-sockets. She slid it into the old-fashioned keyhole and twisted. The locking mechanism popped as it shifted. The door groaned as Morta shoved it open. Dust particles danced in the dim light and Amber sneezed.

"What is this place?" she asked as she stepped past Morta into the final room.

Lamps burst into life. Unlike the white and gold walls of the bar above them, this room's décor was dark. Tapestries hung on the walls, and a massive wooden desk filled the space on one end. A rug made from what appeared to be the hide of a white tiger covered the floor. Bookcases laden with actual books lined the walls. Amber gasped as she twirled around the room. She had never seen a physical book before. The closest she'd come was a 3D hologram. She trailed her fingers over the spine of one. It was rough to the touch and specks of the spine flaked off. She jerked her hand back and gawked at Morta with a mortified expression on her face.

"Careful with that one," the older woman chided. "It's from the mid-2000s."

Amber's lips formed a small 'O' as she looked more closely at the title. The gilded lettering was too faded to read. She tried to remember what her history teacher had said about book production. If she remembered correctly, no new books had been printed since 2471. If what Morta was saying was true, the book she was currently touching was more than a thousand years old. She leaned in closer and noticed the deep, musty smell coming from the books. Wrinkling her nose, she stepped back and narrowed her eyes at Morta.

"How did you get these?"

"I have my ways," she responded as she motioned for Amber to take a seat on a small loveseat nestled against the wall.

She did as she was told.

Morta pushed a tray towards Amber. It was laden with pastries and a teapot.

"How quaint," Amber said as she lifted a cookie from the tray.

Morta smirked at her, her blue eyes flashing. "This room reminds me of simpler times."

Amber bit into the cookie. It was much gooier than she had anticipated and stuck to the roof of her mouth when she tried to swallow.

"I'm at a place in my life where I want to shore up my legacy. As you know, I don't have any children."

Amber gobbled down the cookie and turned her full attention to Morta. There was something in the older woman's voice that wasn't quite right to her. Goosebumps covered her arms and the hair on the back of her neck rose. She rubbed her hands up and down her arms as she waited for Morta to continue.

"I've spent my whole life building this place from the ground up, and now, I want to finalize its dominance. To do that, I need you to help me broker a deal between us and Spade."

"Spade?" She crinkled her nose at the word. "Why would you ever want to work with the LaRues?"

Word on the street was that the LaRues, who owned the third largest business on Thoth, were said to be some of the nastiest business partners. They'd named their gambling syndicate Spade; she had no idea why. She always thought it was to symbolize their desire for power. Their casinos were family-run and functioned more like a seedy gang than anything else. Amber had never considered them to be in the same class as the dark glamor of the Underworld.

Morta sighed and her shoulders sagged almost imperceptibly as she picked up a deck of cards laying on the side table next to where she stood. She shuffled the deck as she moved about the room. "The LaRue family, with all their talk of making it big in the 'V,' are nothing more than a money-hungry mob of dimwitted people. Yet, they have been able to amass nearly as much power as I have." She paused, her breathing ragged as she continued, "They intentionally deny NAs employment. I've heard rumors they funnel investments into Duncan Enterprises in exchange for new biotech," she spat this last sentence as if it were poison.

"Okay. I don't see how any of this would make you want to do business with them," Amber replied. A tremor ran down her spine at the mention of Duncan Enterprises. They were the ones who'd sold faulty tech to NAs when she was still on Earth. She glanced down at the scars scaling her arms. Although tattoos covered most of the damage, she knew they were still there.

Morta stopped shuffling the deck and placed a card, face-up, in Amber's lap. It depicted the king of hearts. Its back revealed a bull wearing a golden crown, encrusted with jewels. There was only one syndicate in the 'V' that used cards with that logo on it.

And it was nearly untouchable.

Amber frowned. She peered into Morta's celestial blue eyes, fearing she knew exactly what her employer intended. There was a fire burning inside them that made her shiver.

"It's impossible," she said, biting her bottom lip. "Even if we were somehow able to negotiate an acquisition of Spade, the King would never let you gain enough power to dethrone him."

Morta chuckled. "Do you honestly think that boy could ever stop me from gaining as much power as I want?"

Amber considered the king of hearts depicted on the card. She had never met the man running the Taurus gambling syndicate, but she had heard the rumors. He'd started out as a dealer in the slums and had worked his way to up the ranks until he was the owner of the most powerful set of gambling rooms on Thoth. He'd done all of this before his fortieth birthday. Her heart thudded against her chest. She had always wanted the chance to meet him.

She shrugged as she dropped the card onto the side table and asked, "What do you want me to do?"

"I have made arrangements for you to meet with members of the LaRue family. You will go as a silent partner. I know you've been practicing your ability to detect others who can manipulate quantum probability. Even for your kind, that's a rare gift. I want you to use it. Manipulate the odds, if you need to, but by the end of the negotiations, I want to be the owner of Spade." She paused for a moment, her breath coming out in heavy, quick puffs. "And, I want you to return that card to the King."

"I can understand wanting to put Spade out of business, but—"

"—But what, girl? Spit it out."

"But," Amber emphasized the word, "Why antagonize the King by waving his calling card around as if you already owned Taurus as well?" Her skin chilled at the question as she anticipated Morta's reaction.

"He'll know what it means."

Amber tapped her finger on the card, contemplating Morta's request. She already knew she'd say yes. She had never declined any of her employer's wishes. Not ever. And, she didn't intend to start now. But, she couldn't ignore the tingling sensation at the nape of her neck or the hair on her arms standing on-end. Although her stabilizers didn't engage, she knew to trust her instincts and they were telling her to be careful.

"Are you sure this is what you want, Morta, to start a war between the syndicates?"

"When you've been alive as long a I have, child, you'll understand why I'm doing this."

Amber shook her head. No one knew how old Morta was. She didn't look like she could be a day past thirty, but she had been the owner of the Underworld for longer than that. Amber had seen the way her wrinkles disappeared and her hair became glossy and soft again following the collection of the souls owed to her. Everyone knew her youth was something linked to her naturally-augmented abilities. Yet, no one knew how.

"I doubt I'll ever live to be as old as you are now," she replied.

Morta ignored Amber's retort. She always did whenever Amber made a comment about her youth or her ability to steal another person's vitality. She called it stealing souls and used her abilities to strike fear in her gamblers. But, Amber had been with the older woman too many times when she'd sucked the energy from another person not to see her abilities as powerful as well as sinister.

"You're either with me, or you're not. The choice is yours. This is not something I ask of you lightly. I know the dangers you may face."

Amber pursed her lips at that. Sure, the LaRues were known for being underhanded, but dangerous? For her? She'd survived worse. What she didn't understand was why it was so important for Morta to establish the Underworld as the preeminent gambling syndicate on Thoth.

"Why is it so important to you to derail the system you helped create here?" she asked. It was a risk; she never knew how Morta would respond to this type of question, but she needed to know.

Morta skimmed her fingers over the tomes filling the bookcases. She pulled one from the shelf and gingerly opened it. She held the book so that the spine was barely open. Even with the tenderness with which Morta cradled the book, its leather crinkled and cracked at being opened.

"There's not much left from the old days on Earth," she said. "Some of these books are one of but a few remaining physical copies. But I've read a great number of speeches and histories. There has been a never-ending cycle of great moments in time followed by periods of squalor. I've seen the atrocities humans have committed over the centuries, encapsulated in these texts as well as the video archives stored digitally. Eventually, something has to give."

Amber watched as Morta trailed her finger down one of the pages in the book she held. Her expression was tender, but there was a hard set to her jaw.

"I still have a dream that, one day, this nation will rise up and live up to its creed, 'We hold these truths to be self-evident: that all men are created equal.' Do you know who said that?" she asked, peering over the top of the book.

Amber didn't have the faintest idea. So much of her time in history lessons focused on the events leading up to the wars, the global unification, and the development of the B-drive that much of ancient history had been neglected.

"There was once a time when people were judged based on the color of their skin, much the same way we are judged based on the inherent talents given to us by our genes. Like us, they were used as test subjects for scientific research. Like us, they were treated as less than human. Like us, they were forced to conform to the norms of others. The man who wrote that speech was named Martin Luther King, Jr, and he fought through his words and peaceful action for the right of each individual to be valued as equal."

Amber rolled her eyes. Of course, she wanted that. All the NAs—Naturally-Augmented—did. But they had already fought and lost a war for equality. Those who still clung to the notion that one day they could be treated as equals were fools. Amber knew they never would be. Not until the ones who weren't Naturally-Augmented had fully mapped their DNA and developed cybernetic technologies to artificially provide them with powers.

"I didn't realize you were so passionate about the revolution," she sighed. She did not want to get roped into a war for justice. It would only end in bloodshed. Besides, they were discussing the acquisition of Spade, not rallying the troops to fight for freedom.

Again, Morta shrugged. "We should never stop fighting for our chance to be free."

Amber closed her eyes and pinched the bridge of her nose. She wasn't in the mood to argue with her. "I guess I just don't see how acquiring Spade and taunting Taurus does the things you're hoping to achieve."

"Dismantling the pipeline between Spade and Duncan Enterprises will do more for the cause than most other things people have tried in recent years. Throwing my dominance over Taurus is just a bonus."

"And this is really what you want?" Amber still wasn't convinced Morta was telling her the whole truth of the matter.

"My dearest girl, there is nothing I want more than to tear down the Spade empire and disrupt Duncan Enterprise's funding of NA research."

Amber trailed her fingers over the tattoo covering her left arm again. She'd gotten it when she'd first arrived on Thoth to cover up the scars caused by a piece of faulty Duncan tech her uncle had purchased for her while still on-Earth. He'd forced her to use it so that she could use her abilities for longer durations of time. She shuddered as she remembered how her veins had felt like they were on fire and her skin blistered the first time she'd used it. Even after the first set of scars, he'd still left the tech implanted in her arm. It was only after she'd arrived on Thoth that she'd been able to afford the tech's removal and the purchase of a stabilizer from Weaver Technologies. They were known for their tech specifically designed to help Naturally Augmented individuals learn how to control their abilities without the negative side-effects.

"I'll help you," she murmured. If she looked closely enough, she could still see the scars beneath the intricate designs of the tattoos. S

Morta smiled broadly. "Excellent."

The hair on Amber's arms bristled before laying flat again. She still felt the tingling sensation rushing through her, but ignored her natural warning system. If she could stop other NAs from going through what she had, it would be worth it.

"I guess this makes me a true rebel now."

"I suppose it does," Morta responded.

Chapter Three

Amber pulled her coat collar tight around her neck and pushed through the crowd of tourists. Cool air kissed her, and her stabilizers hummed beneath her skin, leaving her feeling tingly.

There were still three days left before her meeting with the chosen representatives from Spade, and she had a lot of research to complete before then. With Thoth's nearly zero axial tilt, their planet was in a perpetual state of twilight. However, tonight, Mitus was positioned on the other side of Thoth's singular moon. For a few hours, Thoth would be plunged into total darkness. As was customary, hundreds of guests would attend the annual "Midnight Parties" to ring in the new lunar cycle.

Guests were invited to come in their most audacious attire. Masks and flashy, sparkling jewelry were worn by everyone. Drinks were free as long as you were gambling. Normally, Amber would be in one of the Underworld's clubs or gambling rooms to ensure that the House won as often as naught. Tonight was different. Tonight, Amber would be disguised as a guest and attend Spade's most illustrious party.

She already wore her mask. It was a black lace filigree which had been shaped to her face and fit like a dream. She'd died her dark, chestnut hair violet with streaks of silver and wore a silver gown to match. Long, black gloves concealed the sleeve of tattoos covering her left arm. For good measure, she'd slipped on a gaudy, diamond bracelet. It twinkled each time one of its facets caught in the low light of the streetlamps.

Overwrought gamblers crowded in alley ways and begged passersby for spare credits, 'to change their lives.' Even when she'd been hungry, Amber hadn't resorted to begging in these streets. Call it pride, or an adherence to self-determination, she'd vowed she'd never end up like them. She'd offered services to the local restaurants and learned how to steal food, but she had never expected others to take care of her for nothing. Still, she could understand why so many of them did it, especially the Naturally Augmented.

The undercurrent of fear among the NAs was rampant. At any time they could be picked up by the United Terran Force and sent back to Earth. Or worse, to one of the biotech labs she'd heard rumors about. The idea of being held captive in one of those places sent chills down Amber's spine. Being in the service of her uncle had been difficult enough. She didn't want to imagine what being used as a lab rat would feel like. She was more than just her abilities.

Amber was so lost in her thoughts and memories that she didn't notice the man standing in front of her until it was too late. She slammed into him. Stumbling backwards, she tripped over her dress's train. Heat simmered up her arm as her stabilizer activated.

A tingling sensation crackled through the thin circuit embedded beneath her skin. Behind her, a loud argument broke out between a group of gamblers. Amber couldn't see what happened, but when she finally collapsed to the ground, her fall was broken by one of their bodies.

He groaned as her elbow connected with his nose. She whispered a quick apology as she rolled off him. He moaned loudly, a dark bruise already forming beneath his left eye.

"Are you alright?" the man she'd bumped into asked, drawing her attention to him.

She stared at him in disbelief. He wore an all-red outfit which perfectly showed off his chiseled physique. Horns erupted from his head, and the mask he wore sloped into a long, curved nose. Sparkling jewels had been affixed to the mask at various points, but they only added to the sinister-looking ensemble. He held out a hand for her.

The moment their hands touched, a spark of electricity sped through her. She jerked her hand out of his grasp and turned away from him.

He caught her hand again and pulled her against his chest. He smelled of citrus and vanilla.

For a moment, Amber remained locked in his embrace. She was too stunned to pull away from him as she had before. All of Morta's usual customers knew not to touch her. Knew the soul-sucking queen of the Underworld wouldn't hesitate to taste their essence if she thought her prized employee was being molested.

"I'm so sorry," he stammered. "I wasn't paying attention to where I was going." His voice was velvety and deep. The kind of voice she could listen to for hours. "Are you alright?"

"I'm fine," she muttered as she finally regained enough presence of mind to gently shove him away from her. "You should be more careful." Never mind the fact that Amber had also been too engrossed in her own thoughts to notice the man walking beside her.

"Are you sure you're okay?" he pressed, his lips curling upwards in amusement.

She smirked. "Do I look like I'm broken?"

He blushed. Amber rolled her eyes as she pushed past him and continued what remained of her walk to the casino.

"Pretty girls like you shouldn't wander the streets alone at night," he whispered, just loud enough for her to hear.

She whipped around to face him, but only found an empty bar. A knot formed in her stomach. She wrapped her arms around her shoulders as she promptly turned around and began power walking toward her destination. The hair on the back of her neck stood at attention, and she couldn't help but feel as if she were being followed. Yet, every time she glanced behind her, all she saw were other people milling about. There was no sign of the red-clad man.

Setting her jaw, she continued down the street. She had a job to do, and she couldn't let a mysterious stranger stop her from accomplishing her task. She shrugged, releasing the tension that had built up in her shoulders.

Amber slipped into the LaRue family's casino where their most illustrious guests were invited to attend. The bouncer said nothing to her as she passed by him. His eyes gleamed red with a cat's eye stripe down their middle as she passed.

She grimaced at the obvious use of cybernetic technology. She wondered what ability the eyes gave him. If she were a betting woman—which she wasn't—she would guess that they gave him the ability to shoot lasers from his eyes.

Revelry had already begun. Glass orbs had been positioned all around the room to look like the sun, moon, and stars. They glowed all shades of colors ranging from silver-white to blazing orange. Intricately woven cloth hung from banisters and railings. A fountain at the center of the casino spouted golden glitter instead of water.

The pungent, sharp scent of garlic hit Amber as she entered the space. Mixed with the bitter, yet somehow fruity scent of black onyx cocoa powder and the herbal warmth of sage, the smell of roasted lamb and beef made her mouth water. The LaRue's had the delicacies flown in special from Earth every year for the festival; Amber couldn't even begin to fathom the expense.

People and aliens from across the galaxy intermingled in the large, open casino. A large, bulbous creature with three tentacles on its head slugged past her, leaving behind a trail of glittering mucus. Brass instruments played from an elaborate stage set at the front of the high-stakes room. In the shadowy corners of the casino, vibrant wines glowed softly, casting multi-colored auras on their drinkers. Amber's cheeks heated from the amount of entangled flesh revealed by the wines.

Amber thread her way through the overly-packed room until she was at the bar on the outside of the private gambling room. A guard clad in a black uniform and a devil's mask stood outside the room with a gun holstered at his hip. From what Amber could see, it was one of those calibrated ones Duncan Enterprises had released a few years ago. Instead of bullets, they fired different concentrations of lasers. Morta had refused to equip any of her guards with them, claiming they'd been made from the illegal genetic testing of a select few NAs.

"Can I buy you a drink?" a distinctly masculine voice said from behind her.

She jumped slightly as a cool hand stroked her arm. Her cheeks burned as she glanced in the direction of the speaker.

His dark brown eyes shone in the candlelight. He wore a long cape that stretched over his broad shoulders before draping across his lean torso. Half his face was covered by an intricately designed metal mask in the shape of a fox. His tousled hair was a mixture of chocolate brown, copper, and gold. She sucked in a breath as he bent down and grazed his lips over her knuckles.

"I don't believe I've seen you here before." His breath tickled her skin, leaving a trail of warmth spreading from her neck downward.

"Few have," she replied. There was something about his tone—or was it his eyes—that made her heart flutter. He gave her a half-smile as he raised two fingers toward the bartender, who nodded and scuttled away to do whatever bidding the man had silently commanded.

"I usually know everyone who comes here," he pressed. His voice carried a drawl to it common among the LaRue family.

"Maybe it's the mask," she responded, smirking.

The bartender returned, bearing two large glasses with raspberry-colored wine in them. Amber sniffed at the drink. It carried notes of honey and orchids. She raised an eyebrow at him as she sipped at the wine. It was drier than she had been expecting, but ended with a sweet aftertaste.

He leaned in close to her and wrapped his muscled arm around her waist. "No, I don't believe so," he whispered in her ear.

Her left arm tingled, more insistently this time as his grip tightened. He pinned her arm against her side. The full weight of him pressed against her. She struggled to breathe as he held her close to his chest. Even as her heart raced, she couldn't help but notice the warm, sandalwood scent of him. Wrapping her free arm around him, Amber linked her wrists together. The dual stabilizers she'd had implanted during her time on Thoth initialized, sending a jolt of energy through her body.

Just at that moment, a cat raced across the casino. A server, laden with at least four trays of drinks stumbled over the cat and fell backwards, sending the trays into the air. Glass sprayed as the cups shattered all around them. A spikey shard lodged itself in the man's hand. He grunted, his grip loosening slightly.

She slipped from his grasp and immediately kneed him in the groin. His breath whooshed out of him as he gasped in pain.

"Better luck next time," she hissed as she slipped into the crowd of onlookers.

She rushed past the devil-clad guard at the front of the private gambling room. He didn't even glance at her. He was too busy pressing a cloth over the blood bubbling from a wound in his thigh.

The hair on the back of her neck stood on-end as she raced forward. The stabilizers whirred within her. They had been specially designed by Dr. Mason Weaver of Weaver Biotechnologies. He was known as the father of modern biotech—especially tech created to help NAs control and strengthen their abilities.

Unlike other biotech companies, he was known for treating NAs fairly and respectfully. He was also known for developing the best tech in the galaxy for quality. Amber wasn't exactly sure how they worked. She just knew that when they were both initialized, she could manipulate her "luck" beyond what she was normally capable of doing. She just hoped they wouldn't lose their mojo now.

The moment she passed beyond the doorway, she stumbled down several steps before regaining her balance. Torchlight flickered from sconces on the wall. The stairwell was hot and dark and smelled like burning incense as she clamored down the steps. Unlike the clean, well-lit stairs she'd traveled down with Morta only a few days before, these steps were made of worn stone. They were slick and crumbled beneath her feet. She was reticent to go down them, but didn't see any other option.

She knew she didn't have much time. The stranger from the bar would be following her and, most likely, the guard as well. She quickened her pace. The stairwell just kept going. She began counting the steps. If she lost her footing now, she'd be in real danger of tumbling into the middle of whatever lay beneath her. Morta had asked for one thing: discover what the real motives of the LaRue family were. Amber had failed her. Although she knew she could explain what had happened, she didn't want to face the disappointment in Morta's eyes.

Voices echoed from beneath her, too distorted to understand. She slowed her pace and pressed her back to the stone wall. The stairs ended in a narrow passageway which led forward. Not a single light was on nor a candle lit. Amber shivered again as she realized that she was alone, in a mostly deserted area of Spade, with no one to help her if her powers failed her. They had done so before; she had no doubt they'd do so again.

Her skin tingled as she crept closer to the last step and onto the landing. The passageway had five doors attached to it, each with their own symbol carved into a plaque mounted on the door. She had never seen anything like it.

She trailed her fingers over the smooth wood as she examined the carvings. The lines flowed together in intricate patterns that she found it difficult to believe anyone could make such beauty without the aid of a creative augmentation.

A soft clicking sound drew her attention towards one door in particular. A single line etched into the middle of a triangle was engraved in the door. Leaves wound themselves around the line, giving the design an earthy feel. The symbol felt familiar to her, yet she couldn't remember exactly where she had seen it before.

Amber pressed her ear against the door. The clicking sounded almost mechanical, yet the longer she listened to it, the more irregular it became. There was a loud clang, like metal slamming into metal. Startled, she jumped, and her fist slammed into the door as she attempted to steady herself. She panted hard as her nerves buzzed.

"Hello?" a voice whispered from the other side of the door. "Is there someone there?"

Amber stepped backwards. Her heart galloped as she tried to determine what to do next.

"If someone's there, please talk to me."

The voice faltered. Amber turned back to face the door. She knew she shouldn't risk responding. She was there for one purpose: scope out the LaRue family before the negotiation meeting. That was it. Still, there was a plaintiveness to the tone that she couldn't ignore. She knew what it was like to feel trapped and alone. Of course, this could all be a trap. She wasn't naïve enough to believe everything had happened coincidentally. She hesitated.

"Please." The voice trembled on the word and Amber's heart quaked.

Even through the door, Amber heard the prolonged sigh the person made. She flexed her fingers, one foot headed back the way she'd come and the other pointed towards the door.

There was a shuffling sound followed by a loud bang, as if someone were pounding their head against the door.

"Stupid. I can't believe how stupid I am. No one's coming to help me," the person on the other side of the door wailed.

The voice cracked, and Amber could imagine the tears spilling down the speaker's cheeks. She knew what it was to be alone and afraid. Her fingers trailed over the scars that stretched from her wrist to her elbow on her right arm. No one should have to live through the kind of pain caused by not having someone protecting you.

She crept toward the door and placed her palm flat against it. The person on the other side continued to berate themselves. Their words were so full of sorrow and defeat that Amber found herself wanting to put an end to the person's suffering.

"Hello," she whispered.

Silence. Amber swore she would have been able to hear a pin drop in the middle of a haystack as she waited for the other person to respond.

Just as she opened her mouth to say something else, the other person erupted into a stream of chatter.

"You really are there, aren't you? I knew it. I swear I did. It's so good to hear another person's voice. What's your name? Mine's Mindy. Well, actually it's Minerva, but I don't like that name, so I tell everyone to call me Mindy. Can you talk more, please? Oh, it really is so good to hear your voice. You have simply no idea. Truly. What did you say your name was again?"

Amber snapped her lips shut and took a step back. Her palms turned clammy and sweat beaded on her brow. How was she supposed to respond to the complete need in Mindy's tone? She took another step back, trying to create distance and her foot slipped on the stone. A loud squelching sound ripped through the air.

"Please don't go!" the voice shouted. "I swear I won't talk so much. Promise. It's just been so long since anyone's come here to talk to me. It's always robots that deliver my food. Never humans. And they never stay to chat. Even when I know they're AIs, they never stay."

Mindy sniffled loudly. Amber swallowed hard. This was not part of the plan. Her heart beat rapidly. Dizziness swelled within her and she couldn't think straight. The image of two bodies clinging to one another, their skin covered in sores flashed before her eyes. Amber closed her eyes and forced herself to focus on her breathing. That was a long time ago. It wasn't real. Not now anyway.

When she opened her eyes again, she knew one thing for certain: she needed to get out of this place. Her stabilizers hummed beneath her skin. She told herself this was the right choice. The only one. Still, a voice whispered at the back of her mind that she should help.

But she couldn't. The two bodies remained at the edges of her vision. The smell of slowly rotting flesh filling her nose. She couldn't stay here any longer.

"I'm sorry," Amber whispered before turning on her heel and hurrying back the way she'd came. She didn't care if she ran into the guards. This was all just too weird, even for her.

Mindy's whimpers haunted her as she ran. Amber promised herself that she'd ask Morta if she knew of any reason why the LaRue family would keep prisoners locked in Spade's basement.

She promised herself she'd go back for the girl she'd left behind.

Chapter Four

Amber stared at her reflection in her bedroom mirror. She hated wearing black leather. It was heavy, hot, and clung to her body in the all the places she didn't want it to. Morta thought it made her look more intimidating. And sexy. And sex sells better than anything else. Amber hated it.

The catsuit plunged deep into her cleavage revealing way too much of her body. Even though she was alone, it made her blush. The sleeves ended three-quarters of the way down her arms, revealing the erratic tattoos and scars covering her forearms. Her stabilizers glowed faintly as she trailed her fingers down her right arm. She only hoped she'd be able to influence the negotiation enough to help it go smoothly.

She turned to look at her silhouette in the mirror and stuck out her bottom lip. She would definitely need to discuss her attire with Morta if future meetings with Spade were required.

Sighing, she slipped an electrifying baton into the belt at her waist. If push came to shove and she needed to fight her way out, the baton would be able to incapacitate even the toughest of opponents for the precious moments it would take for her to get the hell out of the meeting room.

When she'd told Morta about Mindy, she'd brushed it off as nothing more than a hallucination brought on by too much hooch. Amber didn't buy it. She'd barely had anything to drink before escaping to the basement. Besides, she wasn't damaged enough to conjure up something like that, even if she had seen her parents' bodies at the edges of her vision. That had been a memory. Mindy had been real.

She hadn't been able to rid her dreams of the girl's whimpers. As she stared at herself in the mirror, she couldn't help but think what the girl was doing now. Was she safe? She hoped so.

She shook her head and put on her game face. Mindy wasn't her responsibility. She couldn't save everyone. If her uncle had taught her anything, it was that. Her alarm buzzed, and she turned from the mirror.

It was time.

Pipes dripped brown, sludge-like water onto the concrete floor as she and the negotiator she'd been paired with made their way towards the meeting place. It was, by far, the slummiest place Amber had ever been, which was saying something considering the places she'd been with her uncle.

The tunnel was narrow with little holes cut through the thick metal to let in the hazy twilight sky. Mist swirled at their feet. The black leather clung to Amber, constricting her breathing uncomfortably. She trailed her fingers along the side of the tunnel. A slight prickling at the base of her skull warned that danger lurked nearby.

Morta called it her "spidey-sense," whatever that meant.

She kept one hand wrapped tightly around the baton at her waist. She didn't trust the LaRue family, especially after what she'd seen in their basement. But, Spade fit into Morta's plans for the Underworld.

And, what Morta wanted, Morta got.

They entered into a wide, open space. Pipes zig-zagged across the ceiling, steam puffing from them in clouds. Amber cracked her neck as she mentally reviewed their plan. Set the terms of the deal. Ensure the LaRue family knew their place in the negotiations. Use her gift to influence the proceedings.

Piece of cake. Really. She'd manipulated so many deals in the past, there was no way this one could go wrong.

Still, her heart beating rapidly in her chest and the prickling at the base of her skull continued. It was like an annoying bug. Swarming around her. Making her mind hum. She thrummed her fingers on her baton and willed herself to calm down.

Boots squeaked on metal, and she turned toward the direction of the sound, her hand tightening on the baton.

"It is so good of you to join us," a smooth drawl said as a man entered the clearing. He wore a black jacket studded with rhinestones. The look immediately made Amber distrust him. They lived on a planet devoted to debauchery of all forms. Rhinestones were not part of that equation, especially when fringe was involved.

"Yes," the negotiator, Jasper, replied. He stuck out his arm to shake hands, but the man only stared down at it, a scowl covering his lips.

"Yes, well, we are waiting for you in the drawing room. Please, follow me." He didn't wait for their response as he shoved past them and turned down a side tunnel.

Amber exchanged a look with Jasper. He sucked in his cheeks and shrugged. This was not part of the plan. She doubted that any good would come of it.

The tingling in her arms and at the base of her skull increased exponentially as they followed the Spade representative. He didn't speak to them as they walked. His movements were stiff and calculated, and Amber began to wonder if he were really a robot. It wasn't uncommon on Thoth. They were easier to control and cost less over time.

He led them through a series of turns that Amber knew she would never be able to replicate if she needed to make a break for it. She would need to rely on her abilities to get her out of this if things went south. The realization did nothing to squash the squirming sensation in her stomach.

Eventually, the tunnel began to ascend at a steep incline. Her calf muscles burned as she pushed herself to climb the last few steps to the top. Jasper wheezed beside her, clearly out of shape. She raised an eyebrow at him when he pulled a small cloth from his pant pocket and wiped sweat from his brow.

"What?" he asked.

She smirked but said nothing as the Spade representative flung open a set of double doors and entered into a room made entirely of glass.

A large table stretched through the exact middle of the room. A chandelier hung from the ceiling, its crystals glimmered in the glow of hundreds of candles.

"We are so pleased to be meeting with you," a woman clad in a violet gown with a plunging neckline said as she rose from her chair. Her chestnut locks tumbled over her shoulders and curled around her face. She was plumper than most of the women on Thoth, but her curves suited her lively eyes and sweet smile.

Clearly, Spade agreed that sex sells.

"Ahem." Amber cleared her throat and stepped forward. She glared at the puppy-dog-eyes Jasper was giving the woman. He didn't seem to notice. "It's great to meet you," she said, thrusting her hand out. "I'm Fortuna. This is—"

"—Thor," Jasper cut in.

Alright, he didn't want his real name being used. Amber could respect that. Very few people—even members of the Underworld—knew her real name. She intended to keep it that way.

"Thor," she repeated. "We are appreciative that this deal is moving forward to the negotiation phase."

"Yes, I'm sure you are," the woman replied, looking Amber up and down. She turned her gaze on Jasper and smiled. "We very much desire to close this deal as quickly as possible."

"That is good to hear," he said, giving a slight bow.

There was something about the girl's tone that made Amber's skin crawl.

"Alright then. We're all on the same page. Let's make this happen," Amber said, placing herself between Jasper and the woman. She didn't like how her stabilizers sizzled beneath her skin at the woman's smile. Her heartrate continued to increase, the erratic thumping echoing in her ears.

The woman pursed her lips. "I'm afraid I haven't been a fabulous host, have I?" she asked. She stared straight into Amber's eyes as she spoke.

By the stars, did this woman ever blink? "It's honestly fine. Just tell us what to call you and the guy," she jerked her head toward the man who had led them to the room.

"Oh, you can call him Sparrow. I'm Guinevere."

"And I'm Frost," a man said jovially as he entered the room, an enhanced pulser pistol strapped to his back. He wore fingerless gloves over his hands. Wavy copper hair fell across his eyes as he whipped up his hand and grasped Amber's. "You must be the unforgettable Fortuna. I've heard so much about you." He held her hand for a moment too long, and she tugged it out of his grasp with a frown.

"You've heard of me?" she asked. She tried so hard to keep a low profile.

"You're only the most famous luck-driver in the Underworld," he replied smoothly. A smirk flashed across his features before he took on a solemn expression. "Of course, you'll understand why Spade needed to bring our own luck-driver to this meeting," he swept his arm towards Guinevere. "Her talent lies in determining if any manipulation is used."

31

Amber's lips twitched at his amicable tone for what was clearly a passive-aggressive threat. Well, she had some thoughts about how Spade ran their operation. She'd be glad when they took control of the syndicate.

Her stabilizers whirred beneath her skin as she contemplated all the ways she could manipulate the deal. The vicious smile spreading across Guinevere's face gave her pause.

A flash of crystalline blue caught her attention. Jerking her head towards it, she saw the pinprick of blue light emanating from Frost's eye and grimaced.

He had a cybernetic eye.

Although cybernetic enhancements had serious limitations compared to the natural abilities embedded in augmented DNA, they could still be dangerous. She'd once seen a cybernetic eye shoot a laser-beam so concentrated, it melted a tungsten door.

Tungsten.

The laser in that eye got over 3,422.22 degrees Celsius.

She didn't want to consider what Frost's eye could do.

He winked at her, a broad smile stretched across his face as he motioned toward the table.

"Please, sit."

She shared another glance with Jasper. He smiled at her and motioned toward the chairs. She didn't know him well. They'd met only a handful of times during Morta's annual staff celebrations but had never talked for more than a few moments. She didn't know if she trusted him to have her back. Her role in this whole affair was compromised.

A thought gnawed at the back of her mind. How did Spade know she'd be at this meeting? Clenching her jaw, she forced her features to soften as she took the seat indicated by Frost. Morta had trusted her to handle this affair.

She would not disappoint her.

"I assume you've read the contract Morta sent over?" she asked. She placed her baton on the table in front of her. If they wanted to make her feel uncomfortable in this space, she'd do the same to them.

Frost smirked at her. "Of course."

"Good. Then we should be able to finalize this deal quickly," she replied. Sweat beaded on her brow. and her stomach tightened as she tried to breathe but was constricted by the tight leather of her catsuit.

"Not so fast," Guinevere said. She slid into the seat next to Frost and trailed her fingers down his back. "The LaRue family has some concerns about the terms outlined by your, uh, employer."

"Of course, they do," Amber grunted. Why did she ever think this catsuit would work out? She felt woozy from the lack of air, and her stabilizers continued to blaze uncomfortably on her forearms.

"What are their concerns?" Jasper asked as he took a seat next to Amber. He placed a hand delicately on her arm and raised an eyebrow at her.

She could take a hint. He didn't like how she was handling the negotiation. Fine. She wasn't supposed to lead the discussion anyway. She turned her attention back to Frost and Guinevere and smiled.

"First, the amount offered must be a joke. Surely Morta wouldn't send such a paltry offer and expect it to be accepted. Honestly, it was almost insulting," Guinevere sighed. Her tone was so monotone that she sounded almost bored with the conversation.

"I am sure that we can come to an agreeable amount," Jasper replied smoothly. There was barely an edge to his words, though Amber picked up on the sourness to his tone in an instant.

Guinevere slid a small piece of paper across the table. "I think you'll agree that this amount is much more in-line with the value purchasing Spade would bring to the Underworld."

Jasper held the paper before him, his eyes bulging slightly. Amber cocked her head at him, and he handed her the slip. Her teeth clenched at the amount listed.

"Do we look like fools to you?" she hissed as she crumpled the paper and dropped it onto the table. "If Spade isn't serious about selling their properties and place on Thoth, then this meeting is over."

She pressed her hands onto the table and pushed herself up. The hair on the back of her neck stood on end as she met Frost's lazy smirk. She would give anything to be able to wipe that expression off his smarmy face.

"There is no need for that. Our employers are quite aware that Morta has much more to gain from them than they are from her. This acquisition will seal the Underworld's place as the top casino on Thoth," Frost said smoothly.

He rose and leaned toward her. He stretched his hand across the narrow table and tucked a stray hair behind Amber's ear. Although she wanted to flinch from the touch, she forced herself to remain still. Acid burned the back of her throat. She swallowed it down and clenched her jaw. The way he continued to lazily smirk at her reminded her too much of her the men her uncle had sold her to. She squeezed her abdominal muscles and glared at him.

"But, the LaRue's have other opportunities they would like to pursue. If Morta doesn't like this evaluation, I'm sure The King would be more than happy to assume control of Spade's assets," he said.

Amber swatted his hand away.

"I would be very careful what you threaten," she growled, her fingers wrapping around the baton on the table. She wondered if he would continue to smirk with the electrified end jammed into his chest. The thought almost made her laugh.

"I could say the same to you, princess," he said.

The crackle of the electric pulse from the baton filled the space as she initialized it.

"Go on then, tempt me to show you just what I'm capable of doing," she entreated.

Jasper laid a firm hand on her arm, pulling the baton down. "May I have a moment alone with my colleague?" he asked.

Amber didn't break eye contact with Frost. His cybernetic eye glowed an icy blue. She wanted to jab the baton into his eye and see how cocky he felt then.

"Of course," Frost replied, the lopsided smirk returning to his lips. "But don't make us wait too long. The LaRue family is not a patient one."

Sparrow, Frost, and Guinevere exited the small room through a metal door at the back. Jasper waited until the door clicked shut before he withdrew his hand from her arm.

"What the hell was that?" he shouted. "We're supposed to be negotiating this deal, not instigating a syndicate war!"

Shame filled her. She'd let her emotions get the best of her. Again. Great. What was she going to tell Morta? She couldn't think about that now. She needed to focus on getting the deal back on track.

"I know," she huffed.

"Do you have any idea what kind of trouble this is going to get us into? Stars' sake, Fortuna."

Amber stared at her hands. She didn't know what had come over her. "I'm sorry," she said. She meant it.

"You better pray that we can still finalize this deal. Morta was explicit with me that she wanted it sealed today. No matter what the cost. She's authorized me for way more than the amount listed on that paper you decided to destroy."

"I got it!" she growled. She didn't need him to reprimand her. She felt lousy enough about her outburst already. "I just don't know how they knew I'd be here."

He looked at her incredulously.

"What?" she asked.

"Seriously, Fortuna, do you have any idea what kind of a legend you are on the dark net?"

"No—"

"—Exactly. You know, for someone who's supposed to know everything that goes on in the Underworld, you're kinda clueless."

She shrugged.

"Look, I'm not trying to cause a problem here. I just think that we need to think about what we came here to do."

Amber sighed. He was right. "Fine," she grumbled. "Let's bring them back in and find out what else the LaRues asked for."

He placed a heavy hand on her shoulder. She resisted the urge to smack him across the cheek with her baton. She did not like being touched without consent. She'd let him get away with gripping her arm earlier, but this was too much.

She glared at him and bared her teeth. "Let go," she hissed.

Jasper cocked his head at her before slowly removing his hand from her shoulder. "I don't know what your deal is, but you're going to have to get over it. You're here to ensure the deal goes smoothly. So far, all I've seen you do is screw it up. Do that again and I'll make sure Morta knows exactly what kind of benefit you bring to the team."

"Touch me again, and I'll rip your arm off," she spat. She knew she was being too harsh on him. He didn't know her. But, she was pissed at herself for rising to Frost's bait and just wanted to get things over with.

He blinked at her. She glared back.

"Let's get this over with," she said.

She strode to the door Spade's team had left through and shoved it open.

"We're ready," she said and turned her back on them.

"While we were waiting for you, we received a call from Justine LaRue," Frost said. Instead of sitting, he leaned casually against one of the walls. "I'm sorry to say that we will have to postpone further conversations until we feel Morta has fully considered the benefits of this acquisition."

"What!" Amber hissed. "We were only in here for a few moments." Her entire body felt warm. She wasn't sure if that was because of the catsuit or the anger building within her, but she didn't care.

"You asked us to leave the table. Deals change when you make that mistake," Frost drawled. He sounded bored.

Amber clenched the baton in her hand, ready to engage it again but Jasper stepped between them.

"Please, tell Justine that we apologize profusely for Fortuna's outburst. She became overly protective of the Underworld's brand. I'm sure the LaRues will understand—"

Frost laughed, cutting Jasper off. "You can quit your groveling. We're not interested today." He pushed off the wall and strode towards the table. Guinevere and Sparrow remained in the hallway. "Next time, I would suggest leaving the luck-driver at home."

Anger boiled in Amber's veins. If there was one thing she hated, it was being judged for her abilities. Even if she had been intending on using them to manipulate the deal, she didn't like being pre-judged for something she hadn't done yet. Besides, they'd brought their own.

She stormed towards Guinevere and pulled the woman into the room. "She's here!" she yelled, jabbing her finger at the woman. "And she's just like me. So, I would suggest that if you don't want a 'luck-driver' here, you should get rid of her, too."

"Get your hands off me, you augg!" Guinevere shrieked, slamming a fist into Amber's cheek.

Her head snapped to the side. All the wooziness she'd felt earlier didn't compare to the confusion that swelled in her now. Her vision blurred as she turned to face the other woman.

"What the hell!" Amber spat. She rubbed the already swelling spot on her cheek. Her stabilizers whirred, their heat uncomfortable. Her stomach fluttered as she realized that her natural self-preservation hadn't kicked in. It was rare for someone to hit her. She could count on one hand how many times this had happened.

Guinevere slapped her again.

Blood bubbled from a split in Amber's lip. She sucked on the copper-tasting liquid and stepped away from the Spade representative. "Stop doing that," she hissed.

"Doing what?" Guinevere asked as she jumped forward and elbowed Amber in the stomach.

Okay. That. Was. Enough.

Amber dove towards the other woman. The impact knocked the wind from Amber's chest. She yanked on Guinevere's hair as she tumbled backwards. There was a satisfying ripping sound as a chunk of the other woman's hair came free.

Serves her right.

Guinevere tripped over a chair. She fell to the floor.

"Ladies, there's no need for this," Frost said, his cybernetic eye pulsing with light.

Amber screamed as she rushed forward and shoved Guinevere's head to the floor. She punched her in the nose. Once. Twice. And then a third time. A soft crunch told her she'd broken her nose.

"Enough." A blast of cold air swept through the room.

Amber wrapped her arms over her head, trying to keep her ears warm. Her breath came out in a visible cloud.

"Guinevere, your presence is no longer needed. Leave," Frost commanded sternly.

Amber sat back, giving her enough space to heave herself to her feet and run.

"Thor, if you don't mind, I'd like a moment alone with Fortuna," he continued, his eye still pulsing.

Jasper glared at her. Amber just shrugged and pressed a finger to the cut on her lip. She didn't care if she'd botched the negotiation. No one called her augg.

Sparrow followed Jasper from the room, leaving her alone with Frost. She didn't like being in the same room alone with him.

She leapt to her feet and put as much space between them as possible.

Crossing her arms over her chest, she scowled at him. "What?" she barked.

He smiled warmly at her then. "I've been waiting for a chance to be alone with you this entire time," he said, stepping towards her.

"What the hell?" she asked. Her cheeks heated at his words, but her head screamed for her to run.

"I said it earlier. You're a legend, Fortuna."

She rolled her eyes at him. "I just do my job and try not to get killed. That last part is normally pretty easy, considering I have a strong sense of self-preservation."

"I can see that." He took another step towards her. "Look, I can tell we've started off on the wrong foot. I would like to remedy that, if I can. But you have to trust me."

She cocked her head at him, one eyebrow raising. There was no way in the stars that she was going to trust him. "You seriously think I can trust you now? No. I don't think so. Better luck next time."

He took another step towards her. She clenched her hands, the stabilizers flaring to life.

"Back off," she commanded. Her entire body tensed as she anticipated his next move. She'd seen his type before. Overconfident. Completely focused on one thing and one thing only. She could normally dispatch them quickly. But they were alone in a secret, underground meeting cavern which left a lot to be desired in terms of escape routes.

He held up his hands plaintively at her, the gesture not quite meeting his eyes. He stared at her hungrily for several seconds before giving her more space. He shoved his hands into his pockets.

"I would very much like for us to be friends," he said.

Well, she could give him one thing. With his tousled hair and relaxed stance, he gave the appearance of not caring about her answer. Yet, there was a tension to his shoulders and a slight tick to his lips that told a different story. She could toy with him, make him feel secure. Maybe even get him to accept terms that benefited the Underworld. She stopped herself from smiling at the thought. Maybe Morta really was right. Sex did sell.

She leaned her back against the wall, the black leather stretching uncomfortably across her abdomen. His eyes narrowed on the cleavage bursting at the top of the catsuit. Men were so predictable.

She smirked. "We can be friends when the acquisition is complete." Too bad Amber wasn't interested in sealing the deal through those means.

The chamber became suddenly cold as a gust of wind swirled around her. She shivered, her eyes narrowing on the hazy blue light emanating from Frost's eye.

"Stop it," she hissed.

He shook his head as if startled, and the breeze dissipated as quickly as it had come. He lowered his gaze to hers and murmured, "Sorry," before backing away from her.

"You don't know how to control it, do you?" she asked before she could stop herself. She'd met plenty of naturally augmented individuals who didn't have anyone to teach them how to use their abilities, but it was rare for someone to become cybernetically enhanced who didn't go through the proper training.

He shrugged.

"It's nothing to be ashamed of," she said. Despite herself, she felt empathy for his situation.

"Says the girl who's a legend," he replied contemptuously. "How could you possibly understand what it's like to be ridiculed by your friends for not having a handle on your abilities?"

Instinctively, she rubbed her hand across her arm where the scarring was the worst. She was always nervous someone would recognize them for what they were: a bad reaction to faulty tech.

She squared her shoulders at him. "We all start somewhere. I'm just surprised the LaRue family would risk sending in someone as," she paused, "uh, untrained as you to handle this big of a negotiation."

"I asked for it."

"Really?"

"It was more like I begged to be assigned to this case."

"Why?" she asked. She couldn't understand it.

He blushed again before shaking his head and meeting her gaze. "I knew there'd be a pretty girl here, and I didn't want to miss my shot."

Heat swelled in her abdomen and she chuckled. In spite of herself, she felt her reservations about him melting away like butter in a frying pan. She was determined to remain guarded around him, but there was something intriguing about him that left her wanting more.

Then she remembered that he'd told Jasper to leave her at home next time, and she seethed.

"If you wanted to meet me so badly, then why did you tell me to stay away for the next meeting."

He smiled at her, his eyebrows raising. "Isn't it obvious?" he asked.

"Umm, no. It's not, actually. Otherwise I wouldn't have asked."

"It was a show. I couldn't have Guinevere or Sparrow report back to the LaRues that I showed you any kind of favoritism. Think about it, Fortuna." He stepped towards her as he spoke. Before she knew what was happening, he'd placed both hands on her shoulders and was staring down at her, a wolfish grin on his face. "If they thought, even for a second that I would compromise Spade's interest during this negotiation or that I let you manipulate me, I'd be floating in the sludge pools."

The hair on the back of her neck prickled slightly at his touch and his words. He sounded earnest. He didn't blink when he met her gaze, and his hands were warm and gentle on her shoulders. Ignoring the mild tingle of her ability's warning, she smiled at him.

"Just so you know, I will be coming back next time. I'd suggest you prepare for it."

His smile deepened. "Of course, Fortuna. As you wish."

They stood like that for a moment before she cleared her throat and stepped away from him.

"Tell the LaRues that we want to meet again in one week," she said.

He nodded once. "I look forward to seeing you again."

"Find a trainer," she said. "Learning to control your abilities is worth it."

"I will," he promised.

She nodded. A smile crept across her face. If nothing else, she could help make a positive change for him. Her heart fluttered slightly at the warmth in his return smile. She shoved down the elation she felt bubbling within her. This was decidedly not what she wanted.

She slipped past him without another word. He didn't try to stop her. She felt his eyes lingering on her as she left. For the slightest of moments, her stabilizers tingled as energy coursed up her arms and a sense of foreboding enveloped her. It passed quickly, and she didn't give it a second thought as she collected Jasper from the tunnel and made her way back to the Underworld.

Chapter Five

Amber twirled a strand of her hair between two fingers as she looked at her cards again. She had a king and a two, both hearts. Scooting several chips forward, she raised the bet. She'd been sitting at this table for well over an hour now, and her fingers had tingled the entire time.

Someone at this table was cheating.

Furtively, she glanced at the rest of the players. One of their regulars sat next to her. He shoved his shades up the bridge of his nose as he stared down at his cards. Sweat rolled down his temples. He'd already lost ten thousand credits during the time Amber had been at the table. He dropped the cards onto the table and called her bid. He was down to the last of his chips. Anymore betting from him could only mean one thing: he'd leave—which Amber doubted—or he'd request a house loan.

Amber swallowed. He clearly wasn't the cheater.

She directed her gaze towards a couple at the other end of the table. She wore a red dress so form fitting, it left little to the imagination. Cutouts around her sides and back gave the impression the dress was little more than strips of fabric tied together. She'd already drank three sangrias while Amber had been at the table, and she giggled every time her partner leaned in to whisper in her ear.

Unlike the woman he was with, the man seemed almost stoic as he observed the game table. He wore a pressed shirt and tie. Muscles strained beneath the fabric when he pushed more chips onto the table to further raise the bet. He'd won several times during the game and Amber couldn't tell if he was just lucky, counting cards, or cheating.

Between the man to her left and the couple across the table sat an older man with white hair and a younger, single female with startling red hair. The older man was another regular. He spent a lot of money on drinks for younger men and women who joined him at tables. On more than one occasion, Amber had seen him convince an unsuspecting beginner to leave with him for the night.

The single female glanced nervously at her cards and then at the dwindling chips before her. She leaned in close to the older man and whispered, "What should I do?" before flashing her cards at him.

Although not strictly forbidden by the Underwold, players showing their cards to other members of the same table was frowned upon by not only Morta, but also the other enforcers scattered across the various tables in the casino. Amber sipped from her wine glass and watched the older man drop his hand onto the woman's back as he peered closer at her cards. His lips curled into a soft smile as he told her to call the bid instead of folding.

The flop followed, and Amber knew that she might have one of the best hands. Two more hearts, a ten and an ace, and the two of spades. She resisted the urge to smile as she shoved a healthy bet forward.

The nervous regular beside her glared, more sweat coating his upper lip. He licked it off, smacking his lips closed again as he glanced between his cards and the ones revealed in the flop. He shoved the remainder of his chips forward.

"All in," he said, gruffly.

Amber tapped her fingers on the table. She couldn't affect what happened during card games as well as she could in something like craps or roulette. But, she could tell if someone else was using an ability to manipulate the odds or straight up cheating. The moment his fingers lifted from the chips, her stabilizers flared to life and a sting of hot pain coursed up her arms.

She caught one of the guard's eyes. She liked him. They'd even gone on a date once. He turned out not to be her type, but he'd been fun. She tucked the strand of hair she'd been playing with behind her ear and rolled her eyes at him. He smirked before casually strolling over and sinking into the empty chair to her right.

He didn't say anything as he placed his chip reader on the table, and the dealer nodded at him. New players had to wait until the end of the hand to enter the game.

As anticipated, the older man called, the younger woman folded, the stern man across the table raised, and his companion also folded. Amber pushed in more of her chips. What the other players at the table didn't know was that she had an unlimited supply of credits to use when working the room. Morta expected her to watch the elite tables during their peak times and sit in the lower grade rooms whenever she could. It was part of her contract.

The man beside her tapped the electronic pad in front of him and signed into his account. Amber averted her eyes as he made a few selections, and the pad went blank again. The dealer counted out another ten thousand chips and pushed them in front of the man.

He ran his fingers over the tops of the chip stacks before finally dividing his new inventory and shoving in a third.

The white-haired man blanched. He looked between his cards and the ones on the table before folding. He leaned in close to the girl and asked her what she wanted to drink.

"Club soda," she responded, a smile dancing across her lips. Smart girl.

Unsurprisingly, the man across from her called.

The turn revealed the queen of diamonds.

Amber did some quick calculations. She still had a good hand, but if someone had a jack, they could have a straight. She still needed another heart to have a flush. The best she had right now was a pair of twos, which wasn't enough.

"Call," she said, sitting back and sighing.

To her surprise, everyone else called, and the river was turned without any additional bids.

Amber's heart dropped when she saw the flash of red as the last card was turned. And then sank deep into the pit of her stomach. It wasn't a heart. Four of diamond.

Her hands shook as she looked at her cards again. Her head ached, and all her senses screamed that there was something else going on. She gripped the sides of her chair as she slipped her cards over to reveal that all she had was a pair of twos.

Arrogant lover had the ten of clubs and the ten of spades. Amber narrowed her eyes at him. He had three of a kind, a decent hand for sure. The tingling sensation in her hands began to burn the longer she stared at him. She couldn't tell if he was the one cheating or not. She nudged the guard, Anthony, as she turned to face the man sitting to her left.

He smirked as he revealed the jack of heart and a king of clubs. Amber scowled at the cards as the heat in her hands grew beyond a comfortably warm sensation to a raging fire. She elbowed the guard in the gut and hoped he would catch her meaning as the regular began to rake in his rewards.

He stood, strode to the spot directly behind the regular, and placed his hands on the man's shoulders. The regular jolted, his eyes bulging from his head.

"What in the stars!" he began as he turned to face Anthony

"Come with me," he said, his face emotionless.

Amber closed her eyes and breathed out slowly. The pounding of her heart in her chest thrummed in her ears as she prayed that the man went quietly.

He wiped sweat from his brow with the back of hand and glared at Anthony.

"Who the hell do you think you are?" he spat.

Anthony flashed his badge, the one all the guards carried with them for this exact reason, before yanking the man out of his chair.

"Put me down!" he yelled. He flailed his arms out, knocking Amber in the back of the in the process.

She was more stunned than hurt.

"You need to come with me," Anthony reiterated. "There's no reason to cause a scene."

The man growled and flung his head background, knocking Anthony straight in the nose. Amber heard the distinctive crunch of his nose breaking. The other women at the table screamed, both leaping to their feet and backing away from the table.

Great.

Amber laid a hand on the man's arm and squeezed gently. She leaned in close and whispered, "Do you know who I am?"

He trembled beneath her grasp, and his breathing hitched. He recognized her. His skin faded into a pale cream, dark bags under his eyes becoming more prominent.

"I didn't do anything wrong," he stammered.

"You and I both know that's not true," she replied. She tightened her grip on his arm.

He sagged beneath her touch. She doubted herself for a moment. It was rare, but there were times when she incorrectly determined who was cheating at a particular table. It made the most sense that the cheater would be him. He'd been losing. He'd just taken out an additional, large sum of credits. And then he'd miraculously won after driving the pot high.

He squirmed beneath her grasp. "Please, I swear I won't do it again."

She closed her eyes and exhaled. She hated when she was right.

"There is nothing I can do for you," she whispered.

Anthony gagged the man with a proficiency that made Amber uncomfortable. He punched the man once, then twice over the temple. Bruises spread across the man's skin, dark and spidery. She looked away.

"Take him to the holding room. I'll send someone to deal with him," she commanded, not meeting Anthony's gaze. He made an affirming sound before throwing the man over his shoulder and slipping from the room.

The room had gone still and silent. The two other women who had been at their table were sitting quietly in their chairs, their skin pale and eyes swollen. Amber rubbed the back of her hands. They were still warm from the stabilizers heating beneath her skin.

Sometimes she wondered what it would be like without the stabilizers to help her control her abilities. She would be stronger, more capable of controlling the world around her, but her abilities would be less predictable. Although her ability wasn't as violent as some of the others she'd seen over the years, it could still be dangerous.

"You certainly have a knack for getting yourself into trouble," a low voice whispered into her ear.

She cocked her head towards him. She'd learned the less she emoted, the more power she retained.

"Have you been watching me?" she asked, a hint of amusement in her voice despite the squirming in her stomach.

He moved to take the seat next to her, and she glanced at the speaker. There was something familiar about him, but she didn't quite know where to place it. His coppery brown hair curled slightly at the ends as he swept a hand through it.

"You're hard to miss," he said as he slipped his hand into his jacket and pulled out a tablet. The retina scanner ignited as he stared into the camera. He held the screen close to his body, and he punched in his security code and handed it to the dealer. "You'll join me for a game," he said.

It wasn't a question.

Amber considered declining. She did need to notify the guard center that there was a new occupant in the holding room. But she also couldn't deny the curiosity brimming within her.

"Who are you?" she asked as she picked up a chip from her pile and began flipping it back-and-forth over her fingers. When he didn't respond, she asked, "Have we met before?"

"I'm hurt you don't remember," he said, pressing his hands to his chest. He looked aghast at her, but his eyes sparkled with mischief. "Then again, it was the reigning of a new year, so who knows how high you were."

It was her turn to pretend to be offended. She didn't drink often and had only tried the psychotropic drugs popular in the casinos when Morta had insisted she understand the substances' effects. She didn't enjoy being called out like this.

"Oh, did I misjudge? It's just that you slammed into me with little regard." He shrugged. His golden-brown eyes smoldered as he lifted one of his chips and placed it before him to enter the game.

"I normally prefer blackjack, but since you were here, I suppose I'll just have to test my luck."

Her back stiffened at the way he said the last three words. She didn't feel in danger, and her ability didn't pulse within her, yet his words left her feeling unsettled. She shoved forward her bet without looking at the two cards dealt to her.

She retraced her steps the night of the new year. There'd been a guard wearing a black outfit and a devil mask and she'd been joined at the bar by a man wearing a fox's mask. She studied his profile as he looked at his cards before raising the bid.

Straight nose; smooth, olive skin that glowed slightly when the light hit it; full, dark eyebrows; a narrow face and chin.

He was handsome, in his tailored clothing. A ruby ring glistened on his finger. She took in his toned shoulders and strong arms. He clearly spent time in a training facility. A silver ring hung from his belt with different items attached to it. Some of them glowed.

"See something you like?" he whispered exaggerated the motion of looking towards his crotch.

Her eyebrows rose, and she felt the heat rise in her cheeks as she quickly turned away from him. Flustered, she wiped her hands on her dress.

He ran a hand down her arm. Electricity exploded in the places his skin met hers. He paused on the place where her tattoos covered the worst of her scars and scowled. Rubbing his thumb over the raised tissue, he met her gaze.

"You should not have had to experience this," he whispered.

She pulled her arm from his grasp and turned her back to him. Her heart leapt in her chest. The way he engaged with her, it felt as if he were looking straight through her. Like he could see into her very soul. And Amber wasn't even sure she believed in souls. For all she knew, they could be nothing more than meat sacks that decayed when the heart stopped pumping.

"Keep my bid as a tip, Rinald," she said as she slipped from her chair. "I won't be back tonight."

She swept what remained of her chips into a small black pouch and stormed from the table. Who did he think he was? She had thought only Morta knew of the scars. She wanted it that way. She didn't want or need their pity. Despite the odds stacked against her, she had been strong enough to get out.

She had survived.

She didn't need a reminder of what she'd come from. They seeped into her dreams almost every night and, despite the reconstructive surgery Morta had paid for, the scars could not be

S.A. McClure

healed. There were too many of them that were too deep and had killed too much of her flesh.

She clenched and unclenched her fists as she wandered around the casino. If she had wanted him to know about her past, she would have told him.

Lost in thought, she didn't pay attention to where she was going. She drifted to the back of the casino and into a secluded area. Round couches formed pods where private conversations could be had. Noise cancellers were installed at each table for that very purpose. She sank into one them and sighed in relief.

"I didn't mean to upset you," a voice said from behind her.

She jumped and smacked her head on the wall. Even lucky people could be clumsy. Go figure. She groaned as she rubbed the back of her head.

"Go away," she said and reached for the other device installed at each table. If engaged, it would form a pod of energy around her, protecting her.

"Please, don't," he said as leaned his head into the section. "If you engage that now, you'll kill me."

"Would serve your right for interrupting my alone time," she hissed. Her thumb hovered the button.

"I didn't mean to make you uncomfortable."

"I never get uncomfortable. I was just done with the game."

He smirked at her. "We both know that's not true."

She rolled her eyes at him. "Yeah, I know."

He stepped into the small section and sat down on the other side of the couch, opposite her.

"What are you doing here?" she asked.

"You intrigue me," he replied simply.

"You barely know me."

He shrugged. "I've heard of you."

She heaved in a deep breath. That was the second time in only a few days that someone had told her that she was noteworthy on this planet. All she wanted was to fly under the radar. She didn't need people coming after her. To use her. She'd had enough of that on Earth. With her uncle. She'd be damned if she let that happen to her here.

"What do you want?" she asked.

He smirked at her. "I would have thought that was obvious."

Okay. Well, then. She narrowed her eyes at him. Most men who wanted to get intimate with her in that way only wanted one of two things: a favor or power.

She was about to politely decline him when a scream broke through the hum of the casino. It sent a shiver down her spine, and she shot to her feet. It sounded close. Too close.

She waited for a second, to see if she'd imagined it—praying that she had. A second blood-curdling scream rang down the hall. This time, Amber didn't hesitate. She ran towards it, the small pulser pistol she carried with her in the casino already in her hand.

Chapter Six

She slipped on the blood pooling on the marble floor. Hissing, she caught herself on an overturned seat cushion. *What the hell happened here?* she thought as she leapt to her feet and around the corner.

The sight before her made her stop in her tracks. She doubled over, a dry heave already wracking her body. There were at least three of them. All women. Their torsos were sliced down the middle. Chunks of hair with pink flesh still attached lay on the floor where they'd been ripped out.

The sour scent of urine and death wafted over her, and she dry heaved again.

"What the hell happened here?" she gasped, clutching at her stomach. She'd seen death. She could still remember the way her parents' decaying bodies smelled after days of being locked in the same room with them. This was something else.

Something brutal.

The man stood silently at her side, his face impassive. She glanced at him, not really expecting a response. He had been with her when the screaming began. He didn't cause this, and there was no possible way for him to know what had happened.

The hair on the back of her neck prickled, and she quickly raised the pulser pistol and pointed it towards the dark corner at the back of the room. Her hands were suddenly dry, her mind focused solely on the spot in the corner.

Bones crunched beneath something big. Amber gulped as her finger depressed the trigger. She exhaled just as a stream of light erupted from the gun. It briefly illuminated the room, revealing more desecrated bodies.

A large, dark mass raced away from the high-velocity dart. The man gripped her arm and tugged her into a tight embrace. The mass slammed into Amber's side as it fled the room and disappeared down the hall. She shoved the man away, firing several shots after whatever had presumably killed these people. One of them struck a reflective mirror and ricocheted into the beast's leg. There was a grinding noise like metal on metal as the beast faltered.

Closing one eye, she aimed straight at its back. She slid her finger along the power gauge until the shot capacity was at its maximum damage. Exhaling at the same time she pulled the trigger, she watched as the last shot zipped through the air in a blur of bright light. It exploded in a cloud of dust and marble as she missed the target. As the dust settled, it was nowhere to be seen.

Whatever that thing was, it was fast. She spun around to face the man.

"I had it," she barked.

"No, you didn't."

Her shoulders shook as she stared up at him. Her stomach was still tight, and her breathing came in short, quick bursts. She narrowed her eyes at him, her lips pressing into a thin line.

"Don't get in my way."

He held up his hands, placating as she stepped into the blood-smeared room. Careful not to step on any of the bits of flesh and bone sprawled across the floor, she searched for any clue as to what the attacker had been. Deep gouges scraped across the walls and floor as if a clawed hand had scratched them. Amber trailed her fingers over the rough metal of one of the cuts.

The sharp edge sliced her finger open, and she hissed. She squeezed her hand tightly and stuck the injured finger in her mouth to stop the bleeding. The pungent copper of her own blood coated her tongue. She stared down at the gouges. She'd never seen marks like these before. And that thing—whatever it was—had been faster than her high-velocity darts. Faster than her ability to manipulate the odds. It was an unsettling realization.

"I've called the authorities," the man said.

Amber whirled on him, her face a tight mask of indifference. "How long until they arrive?" she asked as blankly as she could.

"Soon enough."

She nodded and turned her attention back to the room. She clicked a button on her gun, and a small light clicked on. Moving it back and forth across the walls and floor, she examined the scene. Her stomach continued to roil, but she kept it under wraps. A silvery substance coated the bodies and filled some of the crevices where the walls had been gouged.

She pressed a button on her dress, and a compression box unfolded from a cleverly concealed pocket. She pulled one of the death cards she kept with her and scraped some of the silver substance onto it. Ripping a strip of her dress off, she wrapped the card and substance inside it and slipped it back into her pocket. The compression box folded back up into the size of a silver stud.

"Come on," she said as she walked past the man. "We can't stay here."

He cocked an eyebrow at her. "Why not?" he asked, not moving.

She didn't turn back to look at him as she replied, "Because there's at least six women in there, all mangled, and we are the only other people back here. I don't know about you, but I'm willing to bet they won't believe us when we say we didn't see anything."

"But we did see something."

"Yeah, like they're going to trust that there was some nondescript monster roaming the casino." She stopped long enough to glance back at him. "Stay if you want, but I have more important things to do than waste my time talking to the department."

He hesitated for a moment. She could tell he was struggling to come up with a reason to stay. She didn't care. There was something killing people in the casino, and she needed to let Morta know. She continued down the hallway.

Footfalls padded behind her. A smile tugged at the corners of her lips.

"Follow me. I know where we can go."

Stones glowed fiery orange in the secret room normally reserved for private parties. Amber sealed the door shut and sent an alert through her chip asking Morta to join them. She leaned with her back against the door and sighed heavily.

The coldness of the door was calming. It grounded her. She closed her eyes and let herself forget, for just a moment, about the torn-to-pieces bodies and the thing loose in the casino.

"Are you alright, Fortuna?" the man, she didn't know his name yet, asked. He sat on one of the overstuffed couches in the center of the room. His long legs stretched out before him as he gazed at her with a concerned expression on his face.

She blinked at him and smiled. Warmth bubbled within the depths of her stomach. Although her mind wouldn't stop replaying what she'd seen, it was nice knowing he cared enough to ask how she was. She was too tired to squelch that feeling in the bud. She didn't have time for romance.

"I'm fine," she said as she clipped her pulser pistol back into its holster. She walked over to the couch and sat next to him. "So," she said, picking at a stray thread on the couch cushion, "mind telling me what I should call you?"

He placed a warm hand atop hers. "It's ok if you're not alright," he whispered.

His warm brown eyes had so much light in them that, for a moment, Amber almost trusted him. She jerked her hand out of his and placed it on her hip, right where her pulser pistol was.

"I said I'm fine," she hissed. A muscle in her eye twitched at the lie, but he didn't need to know that. No, what he needed to understand was that she was the one in control of this situation.

"You don't have to be afraid of me," he whispered, leaning in close to her. His eyes fell on her lips.

She resisted the urge to roll her eyes at him. Men were so predictable and, apparently, this one was no different. "Look, if you were hoping to get lucky with me, you would have better odds at the casalarian table." She stood up and moved to the cooler included in the small bar area. "Now," she said as she plucked a bottle of wine—the good kind from the Kalvian system—from the cooler and sifted through a drawer until she found a corkscrew. "Tell me your name."

"Call me J."

She snorted. "Really? That's the best name you could come up with?"

He smirked at her. "For the time being." His brows knit as he leaned towards her and said, "I look forward to learning more about the infamous Fortuna of the Underworld."

Her jaw fell open at his obviously bad come on. "You've got so little game, it's not even funny," she said.

He shrugged, leaning back. "Just testing your reactions."

She poured herself a glass of the wine, downed it, and then poured another one. The sweet liquid turned to fire in her gut. She was thankful for the lightheaded feeling that followed drinking an entire glass so quickly. She didn't want to think about the mangled mass of flesh, bone, and hair anymore. She just wanted to be.

She poured a second one for J and handed it to be him before taking a seat on the chair opposite him.

"Why are you following me?" she asked, sipping from her cup.

"Me? Follow you? You must be kidding."

She narrowed her eyes at him and gave him a look that spoke louder than words ever could.

He smiled lazily at her and said, "I heard that you were having trouble with your negotiations with the LaRues, and I want to offer my services."

She sat back in surprise. How had he even known about the negotiation? Tension began creeping back into her shoulders as she eyed him warily. "Go on," she commanded.

"What if I told you I had some information that would help you acquire Spade from the LaRues?"

"I'd say you were sticking your nose in where it wasn't needed."

He chuckled at her, his smile broadening. "I like you, Fortuna. You're not anything like what I was expecting."

"Oh yeah?" she asked, "And what were you expecting?"

"The way you were described to me was as a cold, hard, ice queen who delighted in delivering the death blows to men."

She glared at him. She did not deliver death blows. Sure, she guaranteed people knew Morta was coming for them when they didn't pay their debts, but that was different.

"Don't look so angry," he said. Warmth exuded from him as he continued, "But then I met you on the new year, and you were so much more interesting than I thought you'd be."

"You remember that very differently than I do," she said, taking a large gulp from her glass. Her skin began to tingle pleasantly as the euphoric effects of the wine began to kick in. Stars, she loved Kalvian wine.

"Morta will be here any moment," he said as he picked up his glass of wine and drained it within a matter of seconds.

Amber stared at him, confused. He slammed the glass back on the table and reached out to grasp her hands in his own. This time, she didn't pull away from him.

"I think we could be great friends, you and I," he whispered as he rubbed his thumb across her knuckles. He leaned down, his lips grazing her ear as he said, "The next time you meet with Frost, be sure to carry this with you."

He dropped a small, yet surprisingly heavy object into her hand before pressing his lips to hers. She was so surprised by the touch of his lips on her own that she didn't pull away from him. She closed her eyes as she leaned into him. His lips were warm and firm, yet tender.

Hungry.

She leaned into the kiss, her heart skipped a beat. Or maybe two. Who was counting? She didn't care. All that mattered was how warm he was on her.

The kiss was over before Amber could think to push him away. Her eyes fluttered open as a small smile crossed her lips.

"What was th—" she stopped mi-word as she realized he was gone.

She searched the room, but he was nowhere to be found. Her stomach felt as if hundreds of ropes had been tied around her middle, constricting her. She breathed in deeply, trying to force the warmth of his lips on hers from her memory. The feel of him lingered.

She pressed a finger to her lips.

Grinding metal sounded from behind her followed by the tell-tale hiss of the air-lock being released as Morta entered the room. Amber slipped the object J had given her behind the pulser pistol. She couldn't explain why she didn't want Morta to know about it; she just knew it was wrong.

She glared at Amber as she stormed into the small space. Amber followed her gaze to the second, empty glass that still lay on the table and blushed.

"You better have a good reason for bringing me here like this," Morta hissed, slamming the door behind her and pressing her thumb against the key lock. It hissed shut with a resounding bang. Morta's special caliber of locks clinked into place as Amber sank into the chair and motioned for Morta to join her.

Morta listened to her tale with an impassive expression on her face. Amber told her everything. About how J had followed her to the secluded room. How the screams had started. How the bodies had looked. And the dark mass.

She got all the way to the wine when she abruptly stopped.

"I can tell there's something else," Morta said lazily. She inspected her nails as if they were the most interesting thing in the room. "Spit it out."

Swallowing, Amber wet her lips. "He told me to be careful the next time I meet with Spade. He seemed particularly interested in helping us finalize the negotiation."

"Is that all?" Morta asked, rolling her eyes towards Amber with a look of distain.

"Why are you acting like what happened tonight isn't a big deal? Do you know what that thing was that killed those women?" Amber leaned towards her employer, her eyes going wide.

"If I had to guess," Morta replied, "I would say that someone has set a shade on us."

"What in the stars is that?" Amber asked. Her heart hammered in her chest.

"So fitting." Morta chuckled. "You know shades were mythical creatures in the old world of Greece? People actually used to think they existed: spirits in the underworld. Clearly someone has been reading the banned books." She twirled a lock of hair between her fingers as she considered.

"Umm, Morta, that doesn't really tell me what that thing was," Amber said. The bands around her stomach continued to tighten as anxiety filled her. Not many in "V" had enough funds to purchase ancient Terran texts.

"Bah," Morta exhaled, drawing her attention back to Amber. "A few years ago there was a new weapon created by Duncan Industries. It's some sort of cybernetic hunter designed to find, capture, and—if needed—kill NAs. They were lab-grown around a metal exoskeleton. They were all supposed to be decommissioned after they started killing not just their targets but innocents as well. The rumor was that something went wrong in their programming."

"So why didn't it kill me?" Amber asked.

"Who knows. You're lucky. Maybe your abilities did their thing." Morta shrugged and leaned back against the couch.

Anxiety continued to storm within Amber as she contemplated telling Morta about the kiss. She decided against it. There were some things she wanted to keep just for herself.

"So, what do we do now? We can't let that thing keep killing people."

Morta nodded her agreement and tapped a finger against her cheek as she thought.

"There are only a few people who could have done this. The LaRues are the most obvious answer, of course. If they can get us backed into a corner, they can negotiate for a higher claim. But, there's also the King."

"He's never involved himself like that before, so why would he now?" Amber asked. The tips of her fingers went numb as she clenched her hands tightly. She didn't know what to think. She was certain that the attack had come from the LaRues.

"Because, if we acquire Spade, then we will be largest syndicate on Thoth. I will dethrone him."

Amber's lips fell into a perfect 'oh.' She hadn't considered this before.

"Well, who do you think the mysterious man was? And how did he get out of here without you seeing him?"

"Those are the best questions you've asked all night, Amber."

"Okay. Thanks for that. But what are your thoughts?"

"I honestly don't know. He could be a plant from Spade, Taurus, or even just someone with a unique interest in you. In us."

"You know I don't like ambiguity, Morta," Amber said with a huff.

"Well, until we find out more about your friend, you're just going to have to deal with it."

The image of the women's dismembered bodies popped into Amber's mind like a bad dream. She closed her eyes, trying to force the memory away.

"And the shade?" she asked through gritted teeth. "What do we do about it?"

"We go hunting," Morta replied, a cold smile spreading across her lips.

Chapter Seven

Amber clutched her pulser pistol in her fist, her finger resting on the trigger as she walked down the hallway with a team of ten mercenaries.

One of them wore a powered armor suit that scratched the marble floor. The large plasma rifle he carried with him must have weighed at least forty kilos. It was powerful enough to knock out an entire ballistic pod wall after only one shot, but it was slow and bulky. Plus, the mercenary encased in the power suit had told her that it could only fire six shots before the capacitor it needed to run had to be recharged.

Was it better to be powerful and slow or weaker and agile? Amber didn't have an answer. She wanted to be both quick and powerful. She needed to be if they were going to complete their mission and take out the shade.

She checked the bracelet dangling from her wrist. Neon numbers flashed on its small screen, indicating the time. They had already been hunting for over an hour. She didn't really understand how they were tracking the beast. One of the mercenaries had explained that the shade emitted a unique heat signature that could be traced using a thermal detector.

Unlike the man wearing the power suit, the rest of them wore standard combat armor. They all bore wearable ballistic shields and had given one to Amber for protection as well. Weaver Technologies created them as part of their defense platform.

Using nith, the toughest metal in the galaxy, nanorobots had been built with the sole purpose of protecting their designated human. The shield had the capacity to block direct blasts from a plasma rifle and withstand several high-velocity darts. She fingered the engagement button as they turned a corner and the commanding officer raised his fist in the air.

Everyone halted.

Amber held the pistol in front of her and slid her finger over the dart selector until the blue indicator light turned orange. She could only hope that armor piercing explosives would work against the shade.

Metal scraped on metal as a large mass shot from the shadows and knocked one of the soldiers standing behind her to the ground. A gurgled cry erupted from the man as his arm was ripped from his shoulder in a spray of crimson blood.

Amber fired once, twice, three times. Her arms shook as the darts shot through the room, leaving a trail of orange mist in their wake. Each one missed their mark by mere millimeters. Cursing, she ducked low to avoid being struck by the deadweight of the fallen mercenary as the shade tossed him across the hallway.

The man wearing the power suit released a bolt of plasma at the shade. The metal walkway heated red before melting where the discharge hit. He, too, had missed the bio-cybernetic weapon.

More men were ripped away from the small band of mercenaries hunting the shade. Screams and blurs of light left Amber feeling disoriented as she released another spray of darts. Although they struck the beast, they glanced off the armored plates covering its back and shoulders. She took in a steadying breath as she reloaded the now empty cartridge.

The shade lunged for the man wearing the power-armor suit just as it released another bolt. The plasma struck the shade in its left shoulder. The scent of charred flesh and molten metal filled the air. The shade screeched as it landed atop the mercenary and began ripping at its armored breastplate.

Metal crunched beneath a powerful strike to the suit's neck brace. Wires sparked as they were severed. The shade wrapped its maw around them and jerked, cleaving the suit's helmet from the rest of the suit.

Her stomach tightened as the smell of fresh blood washed over her. A silent scream erupted from her as the mercenary's head dropped from the helmet and rolled across the floor towards her. She stared into the man's unblinking eyes. She hadn't known his name. She shoved the guilt away and refocused on the fight. If she was going to survive, that's what she needed to do.

Amber exhaled as she fired at the shade. Two of her darts struck the beast right where the plasma blast had. It reared back, and she saw its face for the first time.

Angry, dark eyes stared back at her. Blood dripped from its lips. Although it was humanoid, its teeth were elongated, as if human DNA had been melded with other, more predatory animals. It snarled at her. Pointing the pistol straight at its eye, Amber pulled the trigger. Her arms tingled as she imagined the dart striking one of those eyes and ending the fight.

The shade whipped its head to the side, the dart grazing its ear as it exploded into the wall. She took a step backwards as she ejected the empty cartridge to the ground and pulled a new one from her belt. It howled as it bounded towards her. Her darts grazed the beast's body as it lithely darted from side-to-side to avoid being shot.

Even with her stabilizers whirring beneath her skin, it wasn't enough. She wasn't skilled enough or strong enough to keep up with the shade. Her hands clammy, she reloaded again.

Raising her left arm, she engaged the ballistic shield.

Metal panels fanned out from the brace, forming a barrier large enough to cover her entire body. She held it before her like the lifeline it was as the shade slammed into her. She fell backwards, her head slamming into the ground. Bright light filled her eyes, and she blinked rapidly. The shield vibrated as the nanobots absorbed the force of the shade's strikes. Its weight was crushing, and she realized the only thing preventing her from being completely smashed was the edges of the shield resting on the remnants of the power armor. They provided enough space between the floor and the shield for her body.

A grim smiled passed over her lips. At least her powers were able to protect her from some things.

"Shit," she hissed as a dent began to form in the shield. Her mind was hazy, and she had difficulty breathing. Even with her abilities, she had no idea how she was going to get out of this situation.

With her arm strapped to the shield, there was nowhere for her to go. She closed her eyes, willing her luck to catch up to her circumstances. Heat coursed up and down her arms, as if every nerve in her body were being electrified. The dent deepened as the shade continued to strike the interlocking panels.

She knew the shield would break soon. Once it shattered, there would be nothing to protect her against the shade's attack.

Nothing except her pulser pistol.

Wriggling her shoulders, she carefully pried her right arm from beneath the shield. Thankfully, the pistol hadn't been knocked from her grasp when she fell. Without her right arm adding an additional brace to the shade's weight, the shield applied more pressure to her chest. She coughed as the air was squeezed out of her.

The shade punched the dented metal one more time, and a deep fissure appeared. Cracks rippled across the interlocking panels. They widened as the beast pressed down. The chunks of metal helping prop the shield up groaned beneath the shade's full weight. Metal dust fell into her mouth, and she coughed again.

A loud pop jolted her as one of the shade's claws punctured through the shield's layers. It scraped her abdomen, drawing blood, before receding.

Bursts of light hurt her eyes as plasma bolts and darts exploded against the shade's scaly body.

Lightheaded and wheezing, she angled the pistol towards the hole. She breathed in. Her hand angled slightly as her stabilizers whirred beneath her skin. She focused on the darts passing through the hole unhindered.

Exhaling, she squeezed the trigger and emptied all twenty-five darts. Bursts of orange flame reflected on metal as the darts passed seamlessly through the hole. They exploded in a fiery orange light. The kaboom that followed rattled her skull. The stabilizers died down, her power completely spent. The beast's weight slipped from her broken shield, and she sucked in a deep breath.

Her eyes fluttered shut as the copper and oil sent of the shade's blood trickled in through the hole. Tears leaked from her eyes as its howl sent a shiver down her body. Silence followed as she drifted into the shadows of unconsciousness.

"Get her out of here," a voice growled from above her.

Amber cracked her eyes open, and she groaned. Her body ached from head to toe, and she felt as if her bones had been turned to jelly. Distorted memories of the fight flipped through her mind. The rapid stream of images and color made acid burn the back of her throat. She gagged.

Rough hands slipped beneath her neck and legs and lifted her into the air. Her vision blurry, she couldn't see who cradled her against their chest. At that precise moment, she didn't care.

She was alive.

She was sure she'd broken some bones, and her breathing came out in heavy wheezes, but she didn't care. At least she was breathing at all.

They moved quickly down the hallways. More explosions shook the air around them. The concussive blasts pounded in Amber's head. She snuggled in tighter against the person carrying her, trying to block out the bursts of sound.

"You're going to be alright, Fortuna," a deep male voice whispered.

She recognized that voice. It was familiar to her in the way an old song gets caught in one's mind. It crept along the channel of memory, burrowing into places she didn't know she still remembered.

"Who are you?" she whispered. Her throat ached, and she knew she had been screaming.

He nuzzled his head on top of hers. "Hush, now. You're going to be alright."

She bit back her response to him. Nothing irked her more than when someone refused to answer a direct question. Despite the pain ripping through her body, she squirmed against his grasp.

"Put me down," she grumbled, when he tightened his grip on her.

"I can't do that. Not yet, anyway."

"The stars you can't!" she screamed. She attempted to slap him, but her arm wouldn't respond.

He chuckled when he realized what she was trying to do. "I'm not your enemy, and I'm not going to hurt you. Just calm down."

The words 'calm down' sent a shiver of anger through her. He was officially pushing all her annoyance buttons.

Strangely, the hair on the back of her neck didn't prickle, and her stabilizers didn't react to her desire to leap from his arms. She scrunched her eyes shut and tried to force her abilities to spring to life.

Nothing happened. No flare of fire. No uncomfortable humming in her arms. No tickling sensation at the base of her neck.

Biting her bottom lip, Amber attempted again. Closing her eyes, she focused all her attention on the center of who she was. Morta had taught her that, in order to produce a stronger effect, she needed to practice seeking out the core of her abilities and leveraging that power at will. She was only somewhat skilled at doing this. Most of the time her ability to manipulate the world around her took on a life of its own.

She clenched her teeth as she searched for the spark of her power. She drowned out all other sound and sensation. The stabilizers began to whir beneath her skin as she pulled the ability from the deepest recesses of her mind. She focused the power on a single thought: escape.

Chapter Eight

Shadows crept along the walls as the man continued to carry Amber. She steadied her breathing and calculated what it would take to get away from this man.

She assessed her injuries. Broken arm, probably in multiple locations. Her fingers were numb. Her ribs ached, and her breathing came in short, shallow bursts. She couldn't tell if she was just severely bruised or if she had broken something.

"You shouldn't have accepted this job," the man murmured.

She shifted slightly in his arms, and her spine blazed in agony. Closing her eyes again, she rested her head on his shoulder for a moment. He hadn't killed her yet, and there was no reason to think that he would do so now. She could give herself this moment of reprieve.

"I know you think you can survive anything. Stars, maybe you can. But, Fortuna," he paused for a long second, "your luck can't protect you from everything."

Alright, she thought, *who the hell does he think he is?* Gritting her teeth, she shifted again, hoping to get a better view of his face.

A red scarf was tied around his face, but she could see his eyes. Warm brown eyes.

"J?" she croaked.

He didn't say anything as he clutched her tighter to his chest and pressed his chin on top of her head. Warmth like hot chocolate on a cold day slowly crept through her and she felt herself relaxing. Her mind muddled through the roughness of his shirt, the tenderness of his grasp on her, and the scent of sandalwood and starflowers lingering on his skin. Emotions jumbled together. Excitement. Distress. Fear. Desire. Her need for sleep triumphed over all the others.

She leaned into his embrace. The ache in her muscles receded. Giddiness flowed through her and she giggled softly when he kissed her brow through the scarf.

"I won't let anything harm you," he whispered. "Now sleep."

Her eyelids grew heavy the longer she leaned her head against his shoulder. Although her body longed to drift into the emptiness of sleep, her mind whirred at his words. An uneasiness settled on her stomach. Something wasn't right. The hair on the back of her neck stood on end, and a small shiver wracked her body.

"What are you doing to me?" she mumbled sleepily.

"Hush, Fortuna," he said.

He shifted beneath her, and then his lips were on her own. Too weak to fight against him, she remained still. Despite her reservations, warmth poured through her. The giddiness returned as the kiss lingered. Abruptly, he pulled back and let his hair fall across his features. She couldn't see his expression, only the shadows swarming his face.

Although there was still a part of her that wanted to leap from his grasp and run from him, she remained trapped in his grasp. Euphoria and fear continued to war within her as he stroked his hand down her back. She drifted in and out of sleep.

Simulated bird calls woke her from her slumber. She knew they were simulated because of the regularity of the birdsong and the perfect pitch they obtained. Sometimes, when she was in throes of deepest sleep, she could remember the sound of real birds. Her mother, before her death, loved to leave their apartment window open so they could listen to their songs together. Tears leaked from her eyes as the memory of cool breezes, birdsong, the scent of damp earth and warm vanilla filled her mind.

Wiping the wetness away with the back of her hand, her lips curled into a small smile. Although time cannot heal all wounds, it can lessen the blow. She missed her parents, and there wasn't a day that passed when she didn't wonder what life would have been like if even one of them had survived the plague.

But they hadn't. And she had. And her uncle had taken custody of her. Not even her luck could save her from that.

Absent-mindedly, she trailed her fingers over the scars running like the roots of a great, stubborn tree across her flesh. They were a part of her.

It is the dark times that forge us into who we are meant to be. The words had been her father's, spoken as he lay covered in sores and coughing blood. Her eyes stung for a moment, threatening tears. She closed them, allowing the dull ache of sorrow to touch her for but a moment before resolving not to cry again.

There was no point. Tears did not solve the problems of the world, no matter how good it feels to release them.

Pale orange and gold light slowly crept along the base of the wall, rising and taking shape. It was uncommon for private homes to feature a simulated sunrise. It wasn't much, but it was a clue. She was either in one of the resorts grand enough to afford one or an exclusive mansion located in the ritzy neighborhood reserved for elite guests.

Morta owned one of those houses.

She sat up, the muscles in her spasming as she did so. Memories of the hunt slowly fell into place. The shade had attacked her directly, and it was only her luck that allowed her to survive. She didn't know if the beast still lived.

A light tap on the door drew her attention as Morta stormed into the room.

"Good, you're awake," she said as she sank into the chair near Amber's bed. "I need you to tell me everything that happened down there."

Amber looked at Morta with wide eyes and sighed. Her employer always had been an impatient woman.

"The shade attacked us. I barely survived. The others?" she trailed off, hoping Morta would fill in the gaps.

"Three survived of the ten," she responded, waving her hand dismissively. "The shade was destroyed, thank the gods."

Amber sighed in relief. Although her stomach was still a tangled mass of anxiety and tension, she was thankful that the shade could no longer terrorize innocent people. Her brow furrowed and a dull ache settled into the space between her eyes as she remembered the soldiers' faces. Only three had survived.

"Do you remember anything else about the shade?" Morta leaned forward and placed her hand beneath Amber's chin, drawing her gaze to hers.

Coldness swept through Amber at the question. She remembered its weight as it crushed down upon her and the way it clicked as it moved. Her heart began to beat more rapidly in her chest. She breathed in slowly, willing herself to calm down.

"It was powerful, stronger than anything I've faced before. And it moved fast. Even with my stabilizers engaged, it avoided many of my shots. It was only when it pinned me beneath my ballistic shield that I was able to shoot it."

"I see."

Amber's breathing came in quick, shallow bursts. Her stomach squirmed. She didn't understand who would send such a thing into the heart of the "V." It wasn't just members of the gambling syndicates who lived and worked here. Tourists were here, too. Innocents. Not that she cared. Not much anyway.

"How long have I been out?" she asked, more to distract herself from the memories threatening to break her down than anything else.

"Two days. We postponed the next meeting with Spade so that you can be in attendance. You meet with them again this afternoon."

She opened her mouth to object, but Morta raised a hand, silencing her.

"This is not open for negotiation, Amber. We must secure our assets. I do not want this deal to fall through because of rumors of these attacks."

Amber balled her hands into fists. She didn't want to meet with Frost, Sparrow, or Guinevere again. Besides, she was both physically and emotionally drained. Her abilities would remain in their weakened state until she had time to fully recover from the attack. She wasn't even sure she could manipulate the odds right now, much less fight against Guinevere.

She turned her face away from Morta and stared at the wall. The scent of starflowers and sandalwood lingered on her hair, sending a shiver through her. Had her rescuer told her his name? She couldn't remember. Everything about him was hazy, coated in a indistinct film of euphoria.

"Who brought me here?" she demanded, meeting Morta's gaze. She needed her employer to confirm what her gut was telling her.

"I don't know."

She narrowed her eyes at the other woman. "What do you mean you don't know? How can you not!"

"I found you on one of my couches. You were badly wounded, but had obviously been treated with care. Not even Alex could identify who brought you here."

Amber closed her eyes. Alex, the computer program Morta had designed specifically to manage her estate, was notorious for capturing every visitor's information in great detail. Although not officially classified as an AI, he was so lifelike that Amber sometimes forgot that he was just a program.

At the sound of his name, a soft blue light filled the room as his holograph took shape. He was tall with broad shoulders and wore the type of old suit Amber had only seen in the archives of ancient Earth. He nodded at her.

"There was a glitch in my system at the precise moment you arrived. Data corrupt. I cannot confirm who returned you to us," he said. His voice was monotone, per usual.

"But surely that can't be." Her heart beat rapidly in her chest at his words. If what he was saying was true, then whoever had brought her here knew how to disrupt even the most sophisticated computer programs.

"Indeed, it is," he said, still in that monotone voice. "My system noticed disruption beginning at 0343 hours, which ended at precisely 0350 hours. Not even a shadow of you or the person who brought here can be seen on the footage."

"Let me see it," Amber commanded.

"No," Morta interjected. "Reviewing the footage is a waste of time, Amber. I have already watched them—multiple times—and have discovered nothing. Your time is better spent preparing for the meeting with Spade."

Amber rose unsteadily to her feet. "I think I have a right to—"

"You have a right to nothing, Fortuna."

Morta's use of her street name caused the hair on the back of her neck to stand on-end. Amber stared at her. Her hands shook as anger and fear overwhelmed her. She needed to rationale. To play Morta's game. It was the only way to get what she wanted. And yet, she was finding it increasingly difficult to remain calm.

"Do not forget from whence you came. You were nothing when I found you. I don't regret the kindnesses I've paid you, but do not forget to whom you owe your life. I created this life for you, and I can take it away," Morta continued.

75

Each word was like a stab to Amber's heart. She clenched her jaw so tightly, she thought she would crack a tooth. She was tired, drained, and physically battered. All she wanted to do was rest. To let the numbness take over and drift among her dreams in peace.

Unfortunately, the desire to throat punch someone— preferably Morta—was overpowering. She grasped the blankets in her hands and squeezed to keep herself contained. "I could never forget what you've done for me," she hissed. "But that does not mean I owe you everything. That doesn't mean you own me."

"Well, actually, it does," Morta replied snidely.

Amber blinked rapidly. Her stomach dropped at Morta's words. Hadn't she just compared her to a daughter only a few days ago. Her eyes burned and her lids grew heavy as she stared at Morta. She exhaled, giving herself time control her emotions.

"Alex, can you leave us alone?" she asked, not wanting Morta's program to record their conversation. Morta had a nasty habit of using recordings to win future arguments, and Amber didn't want to give her the opportunity.

Morta nodded her agreement, and the computer program dissipated into a flutter of twinkling light. "Now," she said coldly, "what do you wish to discuss in private?"

Amber fidgeted with her hands as she contemplated exactly how she wanted to phrase her next words. She didn't want to leave any room for interpretation.

"You have shown me more kindness than I deserve," she began. Morta cocked an eyebrow at her, her eyes turning a steely black that made Amber believe that she could never see their depths. "You took me in when no one else would. You helped me learn how to control my abilities. You gave me a home. I can never repay for what you've done." She paused, knowing that the next words would be the ones which would, potentially, chip away at their relationship. "But, I can't do everything you want. I can't be who you want me to be."

"Enough," Morta commanded. She clasped Amber's chin between her finger and thumb and lifted her head until they were eye-to-eye. "Do you know why I am so hard on you?"

"No."

Morta sighed between clenched teeth. "You should know by now that I view you as more than just an employee. You are the daughter I never thought I would have again."

Again? Amber had never heard her employer discuss having a child before. She sat up a little straighter, curious to see what else Morta would reveal about her past. She so rarely spoke about her personal experiences.

"I am grooming you to take over when I'm gone. And these are the sacrifices we must make. You have to learn how to push through the exhaustion, the sheer numbness of witnessing things no human should, to manage our empire."

To Amber's surprise, Morta cupped her cheek and ran her thumb over her skin in a tender caress.

"This casino will be my legacy. As will you."

Amber shivered at Morta's words. Although Morta had hinted at this before, the finality in her tone left Amber feeling numb. She didn't want to control the Underworld. Not if it meant losing Morta.

"I don't—"

"—Stop your excuses," Morta cut her off. "You are recovered enough to do this."

Amber sagged against the pillows. She closed her eyes for a moment, willing herself to sit up again. To fight. To rise to the occasion.

"Fine," she grumbled. "I'll meet with them. But I expect for you to provide me with adequate resources to ensure the deal goes smoothly."

"That's what I have you for," Morta replied as she passed Amber a death card with a single name written across the top.

Amber read the name, her blood turning to ice as she realized just how far Morta was willing to go.

Chapter Nine

Amber trailed her fingers over the name. She knew what it meant. If the deal went awry, Morta expected her to dispose of Frost before he had a chance to communicate with the LaRues. Although she'd found him to be arrogant, he was also intriguing. She didn't want to end his life.

Not yet anyway.

Biting her bottom lip, she slipped the death card into her pocket. There were too many things she didn't have answers to. Who was the girl trapped in the LaRues' basement? Who had sent the shade to kill her? Were they connected? Even though the shade had failed, she didn't feel like they were any closer to getting answers.

She needed answers.

A light rap on the door drew her attention back to the present. This meeting meant everything for the future of the

Underworld. Morta was depending on her. She would rather live an eternity lost in space than let her down.

Jasper remained seated at the table as she rose from her chair and plastered a broad smile on her face. The long, flowing dress she wore glittered softly in the firelight. She'd added a few diamond bracelets to her wrists that clinked together as she held out her hand to Frost.

"It is so good to see you again," she whispered. She tossed her hair over one shoulder, letting her dark locks cascade down her back. Guinevere stepped into the room and snarled. Amber smirked at her.

His lips twitched as he leaned down to kiss the back of her hand. His breath puffed against her skin. Hot. Wet. Oppressive. She cringed and bit back the urge to rip her hand from his grasp. He might be intriguing, but he could also be a snake.

In fact, she was certain he was.

"Are we going to finish this deal, or not?" she asked, slipping her hand from his. She wiped the back of her hand on her dress. The heat of his breath on her skin continued to linger.

He smirked at her and his eyes gleamed as he responded, "Of course."

"Great," she said, taking a seat at the table. She motioned for him to join her.

Guinevere shoved past Frost to take the seat Amber had indicated. She narrowed her eyes at Amber, her nostrils flaring with every breath she took. Frost eased into the chair beside her. His hand slid around her wrist, his fingers tightening their hold. Guinevere looked from his grasp to Amber and slumped against the backrest.

Amber rolled her eyes. They hadn't been in this meeting for longer than three minutes and she was already over it. She tapped the pad sitting on the table in front of her and said, "I have the new offer Morta crafted. We hope it will be to the LaRues liking."

She slid the tablet across the table to him and waited for him to scroll through the multiple page document. His blue eye flashed brilliantly. He clicked a button on the tablet and the screen went dark.

"Morta has authorized all of this?" he asked. His voice hitched, and Amber knew he had been caught off-guard by the offer.

"Yes." She shrugged her shoulders as she spoke. "If the LaRues don't find this deal to their liking, we would like a detailed list of the things they would be willing to accept. Acquiring Spade is our top priority."

She reached across the table and tapped the tablet lightly on the screen. It lit up, and she pressed her thumb against the fingerprint reader to unlock the secret message she'd left hidden on a private window. A little green bubble popped onto the screen.

Frost's brow furrowed as his eyes roamed over the message. He frowned, his eyes darting up to Amber and back down to the tablet.

"Morta cannot be serious," he whispered, shoving the tablet towards Guinevere. "Read that," he commanded, jabbing his finger at the message. His hands shook as he crossed his arms over his chest and glowered.

Guinevere's cheeks paled as she read the message Amber had left for them. She gripped Frost's hand and squeezed. Amber huffed a small laugh at their reactions. It was bad, but not that bad.

"I think that makes our position clear," Amber said as she slipped her baton from its holster and laid it on the table.

"You think threats like this will earn you the LaRues' respect?" Guinevere spat. She gripped her own baton in her hand, the electric charge already sizzling as she drew it up and pointed it at Amber. "It won't."

Amber shrugged again. "I'm sure you can understand my predicament. Morta wants Spade. And I want what Morta wants."

"You're bluffing," Frost snarled at her.

"Am I?" She picked up the baton and twirled it in her hand. Blue light sizzled at one end as she initialized the charge. A blue haze lit up his features as she swung it close to his face. A muscle in his human eye twitched and pucker lines crept out from his lips as he sneered at her.

She winked. "I'm sure Morta would enjoy extracting payment for our time, should it come to that."

His cybernetic eye flashed a brilliant blue as it trailed down her face and scrolled across the message again. His fingers trailed over his jawline. "I'll need a moment to confer with Justine," he said gruffly.

His voice pitched at the end of his phrase, and Amber felt the stirrings of remorse swoop through her chest. She shoved the emotion down like the fly it was and grinned at him. "Of course."

Motioning for Jasper to follow her, she slipped from the room.

Jasper gripped her arm firmly in his grasp the moment the door slid shut behind them.

"What was all that about?" he demanded. His fingers dug into her skin, leaving bruises in their wake.

"What, you didn't know that Morta approved me to make a special amendment to the deal?" she asked, raising an eyebrow at him.

His nostrils flared and his grip on her arm momentarily tightened before relaxing. "No," he replied sheepishly.

She rolled her eyes at him.

"Morta didn't trust you to deliver the message. Why would she? You've never had to tell someone they were going to die by her hand before."

He blanched. "You did what!"

She lifted her chin defiantly at him and stared straight into his eyes as she said, "I delivered the message that if the LaRues decide to pull out of this deal, Morta will find and kill them, one-by-one, until there are none left as compensation for her time."

He blinked at her for several seconds without speaking. Her chest constricted and her breathing became shallower as she waited for him to respond. A dull thudding pounded at the back of her head and she wished that she could curl into a ball and nestle under a set of blankets.

She inhaled deeply, letting the pressure build in her lungs until it felt as if she were going to explode. Her fingertips numbed as she squeezed her hands together and forced herself to smile at him. This is how she survived.

"Why would you agree to that?"

"I'm a blood-thirsty bitch who enjoys destroying others. What can I say?" She smirked at him. Tendrils of doubt curled around her heart and squeezed. She lifted her chin higher. She would give him no reason to doubt her confidence in following Morta's orders, even if queasiness roiled in her stomach.

He glared at her. "What in the stars does that even mean?" He paused and then jabbed his finger at her chest. "Stars, Fortuna! Do you even know what you've done?" His breathing was so heavy that it made her skin crawl to hear him.

She sighed, her shoulders sagging. "Look, Jasper, I know that you're still angry from our last meeting with Spade, and maybe you have every right to be, but this was a direct order from Morta. You know I couldn't refuse."

He held her gaze for several seconds. The tightness in her chest thickened the longer he stared her down. She swallowed hard and blinked. He was already looking away when she opened her eyes again.

She placed a hand on his forearm, and he flinched away from her. She scowled at him. Raging fire coursed through her veins at his rejection.

"Seriously?" she could barely contain the venom from seeping into her voice. "I thought you, of all people, might understand what it's like to receive an order from Morta directly. I'm sorry that she didn't choose you, okay? I'm sorry that I am always the one who gets stuck doing the dirty work because she knows I can basically manipulate my way out of anything. Last time, I was unprepared for Guinevere. This time I wasn't. So," she paused to take a breath. "So, you can just shove it, alright? I haven't done anything wrong."

He released a puffing sound and turned away from her. "Whatever you say, Fortuna. This is your game now. I'm just here to make sure you don't get us both killed."

She stood behind him, shaking. Who the hell did he think he was? Did he even realize all the things she'd been through in the past week? She'd almost died, for stars' sake. And here he was, acting all angry, as if she were the problem. She crossed her arms over her chest.

Jasper slammed his palm onto the door's scanner with a loud bang. The metal frame shook before flashing green. The door slid open with soft grinding sound. Jasper stepped back into the room without looking back at her. Amber clenched her hands, the tightness in her chest painful, as she followed.

Frost was alone at the table. His blue eye glowed brightly as she took her seat again. His features were a mask of placidity. Jasper went to stand in a corner, his arms crossed over his chest. He glowered at her when Amber glanced at him.

"You will be happy to know that Justine has approved all of Morta's terms," Frost whispered. His voice was barely audible across the table, but it was so cold, Amber could imagine it slicing right through her. "Except one."

She cocked an eyebrow at him. "Except one?"

"She wants thirty days to close out her accounts and let her special clients know that the doors to Spade will no longer be owned by the LaRues."

"That's double what Morta asked for!" Amber slammed her fists on the table. She kicked back her seat as she rose. Leaning across the table she snarled at him. Her stabilizers whirred as she imagined fighting with him. Her body wanted to respond. Her mind hesitated.

"Yes, and your master ordered you to kill them all if she didn't comply, so I don't really think you have a reason to be upset that they're simply asking for more time."

She clenched and unclenched her hands. She wasn't sure Morta would approve that long to officially close. She stole a glance at Jasper, but he steadfastly avoided her eyes.

"And the LaRues have agreed to everything else we asked for?" she confirmed.

Frost nodded.

"And they're willing to sign off on the agreement today? To lock it in, with no further negotiation?"

He sighed. "Yes, Fortuna, they're willing to agree to everything else today. The signed agreement will be sent to both set of lawyers for filing."

She held her breath, waiting for her 'spidey-sense' to kick in.

Nothing happened.

The corners of her mouth perked slightly. This wasn't a trick. There was no way Guinevere would be able to stop her innate abilities from warning her off. This was real.

They had won.

She sank back into her seat, a smug smile stretched across her face. "It seems we have a deal."

Chapter Ten

"Are you really sure you want to host an elaborate party now?" Amber asked as she held up a slinky black dress that looked to be about three sizes too small. It sparkled slightly as it reflected the overhead light. She tossed it over her shoulder as she reached for the next one.

Morta's apartment had an entire closet dedicated to just dresses. Most of them were low-cut and form-fitting. Sexy, just the way Morta liked them.

Morta's apartment was a mixture of dark, Terran relics and posh decorations. Candles burned in sconces on the wall. Their flickering light sent shadows writhing across the room. A giant chandelier glittered in the dressing room. Crown molding cased the room.

"Yes," Morta replied, stepping out from behind the changing screen across the room.

Amber gasped slightly at the dress her employer wore. It shimmered silver with each of Morta's movements. It hugged her slender middle and accentuated her bosom before flowing out in a fuller skirt. Little silver butterflies fluttered over the layers of fabric on the skirt.

"What?" Morta asked, stopping in her tracks when she noticed Amber's expression.

Amber wiped her hand over her face. "Nothing. It's just that, I don't think I've ever seen you wear something as gorgeous as that dress."

"It's just a dress, Amber. The real power lies in the person wearing it." She winked at her, a sly smile cresting her lips. "Besides, I want everyone to know who the real queen of Thoth is."

Amber watched as she riffled through the drawers of her dresser. Jewels sparkled as they caught the light. The various pieces clinked as they struck one another. Although she'd been allowed to gaze longingly at the jewelry, she'd never been allowed to wear any of it.

Morta withdrew a box from the deepest drawer at the bottom of the dresser. It was simple, even plain. Dust puffed from it as she removed the lid and reached inside. Amber leaned forward, anxious to catch a glimpse of the treasure the box held. She held her breath as Morta lifted a velvet bag and weighed it in her hand.

Her eyes widened when she saw the crown Morta withdrew from it. Delicate strands of silver wove in and out of each other, forming a knotted, swirling pattern on the sides of the crown. It curved downward at the front, coming to a peak with a small skull with opal eyes at its center. The back of the crown was a mixture of silver strands and opals, arranged in floral pattern.

She placed the crown on her brow and twirled around to see Amber's expression.

Amber stood for several moments, her lips slightly ajar. There was no doubt about it. Morta was one of, if not the, most beautiful people she had ever met. Tonight, she looked like a queen.

"Stop gaping," Morta commanded. "And show me what you intend to wear. Tonight may be a celebration of our deal with Spade, but it is also a declaration of the future."

Her features darkened as she spoke, and Amber wondered what secrets she still had. No matter how close they were or what Morta revealed to her, Amber never felt like she ever really knew her employer. She was an enigma. Maybe she always would be.

"This place has been a cesspool of crimes against the Naturally Augmented for too long. I intend to see that end."

Amber jerked her head towards Morta. "What are you talking about."

Morta didn't reply. Instead, she reached into her closet and pulled a ruby, lace gown. It didn't look like it had a lining to it.

"Wear this one," she said, thrusting the dress at Amber. She stalked over to her dressing table and retrieved a pair of dangling diamond earrings. "And these."

Amber accepted the items with a shaky hand. Memories of the last party she'd been to filled her mind and she gulped. They still hadn't discussed the girl trapped in Spade's basement.

"Umm, Morta, I've been meaning to ask you..." She trailed off, unsure of how to broach the subject again.

Morta glanced at the grandmother clock against the wall. It chimed softly as it reached three-quarters of an hour. Her nose wrinkled in distaste as she turned her attention on Amber. "Spit it out. Our guests will be arriving soon, and I want to make my entrance at the exact right moment."

Amber cringed at Morta's reaction, but knew she couldn't let something as diminutive as fear stop her from continuing.

"I was wondering if we could discuss everything that's been going on again. Who was the girl locked in Spade's basement? Or, at least, why did they have her locked down there? Why would someone send the shade to kill us? None of it makes sense!" Once she started, she found she couldn't stop.

"Amber, it is not the correct time to answer those questions. I'm sorry, but this conversation will have to wait."

Frustration roiled within her. She didn't know why Morta refused to answer her questions, but she would be damned if she let her off the hook that easily. She'd nearly died at the shade's hand. She'd been having nightmares about the girl for days. And, to top it all off, she couldn't shake the feeling that Morta knew more than she was letting on.

"Why won't you just tell me!" She dropped the dress and the earrings to the floor as she strode toward her. By the time she reached Morta, her anger had reduced to the meagerest of morsels. She stammered over her next words. "You keep things from me when all I want is to be of service to you. To this place. Don't you understand that?"

Morta took a step back. Her features remained unphased as she patted down her dress and turned on her heel to walk away.

"Don't turn your back on me, Morta!" Amber screamed.

She glanced over her shoulder at Amber and smirked. "My dear girl, I can do whatever it is I please. I'm the queen now."

Amber gaped after her as she exited her chambers. She waited until she could no longer hear her footsteps before sinking to the floor and letting the tears that had been building cascade down her cheeks. She'd been a fool to think that she could ever persuade her employer to tell her something she clearly had no interest in sharing.

She remained like that for several moments. Her head ached by the time she stopped crying, and her shoulders and back were tense. Pinching the bridge on her nose she counted backwards from ten as she waited for the pressure to subside.

Checking her bracelet, she scrambled to her feet. The party was about to start, and she was expected to be in the high roller room before it began. She changed quickly. The lace dress clung to her curves. It hit her legs mid-thigh, but she knew it would ride up when she sat. Holes between the floral designs in the dress revealed her tanned skin beneath it. She scowled at her reflection in the mirror.

Closing her eyes, she envisioned the person she knew Morta wanted her to be. Flirty. Sensual. Witty.

She always played her part well.

Tonight would be no different.

The earrings were a perfect match for the dress, making her appear older and way more sophisticated than she actually was. Since the encounter with the shade, she'd lost so much weight that the hollows of her cheeks were visible and her collarbone was prominent beneath the curve of her dress. She doubted anyone at the party would notice the gauntness to her bones or the sadness in her eyes. People tend to overlook the things they would rather not see.

She smiled at herself in the mirror before applying a few touchups to her makeup. She would appear flawless to every scumbag in the place. Some of them would have the balls to approach her, but most would be too scared to make a pass. It was better that way. She could focus on her work.

Slipping through the crowd, she made her way to the back of the casino, where the high roller room had been setup, complete with champagne, chocolate-covered strawberries, and men and women who had been paid handsomely to distract the players with lively conversation and sexy flirtation.

She was just about to open the door when a firm hand wrapped around her wrist and yanked her back. She dug her nails into his hand and hissed, bringing her free elbow up to hit her assailant in the solar plexus.

He gasped for air as Amber jammed her foot straight into his instep. He groaned as she threw her hand up and into his nose. She didn't hear it break, but the satisfying gush of blood put a genuine smile on her face. She finished by kneeing him in the groin.

"Morta taught me how to sing," she said as the man dropped to his knees on the ground.

His warm brown eyes met her, and she faltered.

"YOU!" she hissed, bringing her arm up to strike him again. "What are you doing here?"

"Personal invitation," he gasped. His nose continued to trickle blood.

For a moment, Amber almost felt pity for him. It was quickly replaced by annoyance. "I highly doubt Morta personally invited you to the party, J."

He pulled out the small black card with roses scrolling across the border. Silver filigree made it glisten as he showed her where Morta had signed the card.

"You know she has a stamp for that, right?" Amber asked with a smirk.

"Figures," he replied, rolling his eyes.

She suddenly felt awkward standing in front of him as he continued to bleed over his tux. He had saved her life, after all.

She held her hand out to him. He didn't even hesitate as he reached up and grasped her hand in his own. She pulled him to his feet and guided him to the staff room.

"Wait here," she commanded as she went to retrieve a first aid kit from behind one of the bars. Most of them contained the weird goo used by the medics to close and heal wounds.

"Really, I'm fine, Fortuna. There's no need—"

She found the spray can of healing goo just as he finished, "— I'm fine."

To her surprise, the bleeding had stopped of its own accord. The bruise that had previously spotted his cheek where her elbow had connected with the soft spot just below the eye was gone.

"How did you—" she stammered.

He shrugged. "How are you the luckiest woman I've ever met?"

She rolled her eyes at him. "Flattery won't get you anywhere," she said. "But I thought you could control the weather." She thought back to the first time she'd met him. Hadn't he controlled the winds? Now she wasn't so sure.

"Oh, that," he shrugged, "that was nothing compared to what I can really do."

She glanced at him, trying to determine if he was joking with her or not. A small dimple formed in his cheek as he smiled at her.

"So, what led to my employer inviting you to this party?" she asked, her curiosity getting the better of her.

"Well, if I'm being honest, I don't exactly know."

She didn't believe him. Not for a second. "What do you want here, J?" she asked. She sounded cold, even to herself. She valued honesty over anything else. Except for ice cream. Nothing was more important than ice cream.

He smiled at her, bemusement shining in his eyes as he leaned down and placed his hands on the wall to either side of her head. She pressed herself against the wall, her insides squirming at being pinned by him. His lips tickled her ear as he whispered, "I came here to see you again."

His words left her feeling hot. She squelched that feeling as much as she could, but it clung to her like a spiderweb in early morning dew.

"You look ravishing in that dress," he continued as he skimmed his knuckles over her cheeks. He kissed her forehead, letting his lips linger just long enough for her heartbeat to increase to a racing speed.

Unconsciously, she leaned into him. A part of her hungered for his warmth. Her lips parted slightly as she tilted her chin up towards him.

He stepped away, creating a vacuum of space between them that felt like an ice wall. She shook her head, regaining control of herself as she stared at him.

"I wasn't lying," he said. "I came to see you."

Spade

"Why?"

"There's something I think you should see," he replied as he stretched out his hand for her to take.

Her fingers curled inward as she fought the impulse to take his hand. She refused to be one of those girls that turned to mush the minute a handsome guy walked into the room, that she kind of, sort of, maybe liked. That wasn't her.

"Then show me," she said, crossing her arms of her chest and tucking her hands beneath her armpits.

He chuckled at her but didn't force the issue.

He guided her back through the casino, towards the front entrance.

"Umm, J, I know you want to be all secretive and mysterious here, but I need to remind you that I can't leave the Underworld. Not tonight."

He turned towards her then, the smile wiped from his face. When she didn't budge, he sidled over to her and pulled her against the wall. Their bodies were so close, Amber didn't think even a piece of paper could fit between them.

"What are you doing?" she breathed, turning her face away from him. She knew that if she met his gaze or looked at his lips that she would be done for.

"Pretend like you're enjoying yourself so that no one pays attention to us," he hissed at her.

She paused for a second as his words sank in. Then, she wrapped her arms around his back and began moving them up and down his spine, as if the only thing keeping her grounded was his support. It wasn't far from the truth.

"Tell me what's going on," she growled at him through clenched teeth.

"Do you want to know about the people Spade locks in their basement or not?" he asked, his lips grazing her cheeks as he spoke.

"You're joking, right?" she asked. Her palms turned clammy at his words. How had he known about the girl locked in the basement?

"Do I look like someone who would joke about something as serious as that?" he responded, staring her straight in the eyes.

She gulped. He didn't. But then, she didn't really know him that well. She wasn't sure she could trust him. Not yet anyway.

"Could you tell me what you know instead of showing me?"

"No."

"And it has to be tonight?" she asked, already knowing what his response would be.

"Yes."

She clenched and unclenched her hands as she thought about his words. She could go with him. See what he had to show her. And then come back. It was busy enough that no one would notice if their chief anti-cheater left for a few hours, right?

She glanced around the casino as she considered his offer. She could either get answers from J or wait for Morta to trust her enough to tell her the truth. The queasy, unsettled feeling from their conversation earlier that evening pulsed within her. She needed the truth.

"Fine," she snarled. "I'll go with you."

His sigh of relief was palpable.

"But on only one condition," she countered.

"And what's that?"

"You promise to tell me anything I want to know."

"Within reason, sure."

"No, I want to know everything," she said. "You're the tutor," she continued, "teach."

He smirked at her. "Good. You catch on quickly." He brushed a stray strand of hair from her face and leaned into her once more. "I think we're going to get along quite nicely."

"Maybe. Or maybe I'll kill you in your sleep and make it look like a suicide."

He chuckled at her again. Despite herself, she kind of liked his laugh.

"You're dark, but I like it," he said as he tugged her towards the door. "Now, let's go show you what's really been going on in Spade."

Chapter Eleven

No one stopped them as J led her through a series of back alleys and through the V's slums. Greenish-brown slime coated the metal walkways. The smell was worse than the sight. Amber kept sniffing her own hair to keep herself from retching.

"How much farther is it?" she asked.

Instead of responding, he gripped her elbow and turned her towards a dilapidated building at the end of a street. Broken windows stared out at the empty driveway, vacant and Although there was no wind, it seemed to sway as they strode down the pathway to the door.

"Watch your step," he said as he leapt over a hole on the porch. He smiled back at her when she did the same.

The stench of the main room was overpowering. While on Earth, Amber had smelled a lot of foul things. She'd had to remain in the room where her parents had died for days before someone came to help them. She didn't think she could ever forget the way the flies had started to swarm around her mother's rotting body or the smell of flesh slowing decaying.

Somehow, this was worse.

She gagged. Bile swelled in her throat, threatening to suffocate her if not released. She swallowed hard and pressed her nose into the length of her hair. Not even that was enough to stop the scent from permeating every part of her.

"Where in the stars did you bring me?" she seethed.

He held up a single finger to his lips as he helped her navigate over the rotten floorboards of the small house. She had the feeling that he was taking her someplace she would never be able to forget.

The buzz of insects hummed at the back of her mind. She scanned the rooms, searching for their source, knowing this place was death. Closing her eyes, she prayed that whatever it was J wanted to show her wouldn't scar her for life. Well, at least not more than she already was.

He pulled a small, flat disc from his jacket pocket and depressed a groove at its top. It began to glow a soft blue color. Using it to light their way, he continued to lead her further into the house. It was bigger than she had thought from the outside. Each room was styled the way she remembered the house on Earth being. Concrete walls. Little adornment. Almost sterile.

"What is this place?" she asked as they rounded a corner and came to a locked door.

"This is where Spade dumps the things they find undesirable."

Amber didn't know what he meant by that. Why wouldn't they just place them in the trash collector if they didn't want them? Why have an entire house dedicated to 'dumping' them? She opened her mouth to ask additional questions when she heard the hiss of the door opening, and the overwhelming stench of death stopped her in her tracks.

He thrust the orb of light into the room, and Amber nearly collapsed at the sight.

Dead bodies were piled atop one another in different stages of decay. Blood coated the floor where some of them had bled out, apparently still alive when they were left here. There were too many to count. Too many to name.

Tears filled her eyes the longer she stared at the massacre.

"What happened here?" she managed to stutter.

He didn't immediately answer. She closed her eyes, willing the tears to remain locked inside. She couldn't show him that kind of weakness. She didn't want anyone to see it in her.

"I told you. Once Spade decides that something isn't valuable to them anymore, they get rid of it."

She spun on him then. She couldn't believe that he was describing these people as things. Objects owned by, of all things, a gambling syndicate. They had been people. Just like him. Just like her.

She jabbed her finger in his chest, her eyes gleaming with her tears as she freely let them spill down her cheeks. "Who in the stars do you think you are? Huh? Can't you show a little respect to the dead?"

She turned away from him, hurriedly wiping away the tears. She knew the damage was already done, but she didn't care. Her shoulders shook as she thought of all the other things she wanted to say to him. He was a coward, bringing her here like this. what was she supposed to do about it? She was just the person Morta had assigned to deliver the death cards and ensure that no one was cheating in the high roller room.

Nothing more.

"Why did you bring me here?" she whispered. Her anger fled from her like a rabbit being chased by the wolf.

He laid a warm, comforting hand upon her shoulder before speaking. "I thought you needed to see what was at stake. All these people. They were like us. Special."

"They were Naturally Augmented?" Amber asked, turning to look J in the eyes. He nodded once, the only confirmation she

97

needed. She sucked in a deep breath. There were so many. She hadn't even realized there were so many of them living on Thoth.

"Why would Morta keep this from me?" she asked. She didn't expect an answer.

"I think she was trying to protect you," he said as he moved his hand across her back until he was enveloping her in a one-armed hug.

"Yeah, right. Like I would ever believe that. Morta has never once, in all my time working for her, tried to protect me. If anything, she puts me in the line of danger more than anything else. Remember the shade?"

He shrugged. "She works in mysterious ways, but I think it would be beneficial for you to trust her. I don't think she was lying to you to hurt you."

Amber cocked an eyebrow at him. "Why are you defending her?" she asked. She wracked her brain for any plausible explanation. Only one came to mind. "You work for her, is that it?"

He laughed, shaking his head. "No, it's nothing like that. She's just an old acquaintance of mine, and I trust her."

Well, that didn't make her trust him. Morta didn't have 'old,' mysterious acquaintances. She had people she used to achieve her goals. And people she controlled through fear or owed favors. In either case, Amber wouldn't consider them acquaintances.

She forced herself to look at the corpses again. There was a girl, who couldn't have been older than twelve or thirteen, who stared at her with eyes wide open. They were glassy and unseeing. Her throat was bruised and her skin pale, as if she had been drained of all her blood. Dark flakes clung to her neck around the torn flesh. Amber couldn't stop herself from staring at the girl.

She was so young. Too young to have lost her life like this.

Amber turned towards J, her hands balled into fists. "We have to stop this. We have to."

He met her gaze. His eyes were tender and full of life, so unlike the girl in the room. She froze as he cupped her cheek and said, "We will. Together, I think we can do anything."

They remained like that for a few moments before Amber took a step back. The break in contact left her feeling cold. "Why haven't you gone to the authorities?" she asked. Despite her deep mistrust of the Planetary Guard Force, she couldn't understand why Morta had allowed these people to continue being slaughtered like cattle.

J sighed, his shoulders slumping. "They're owned by the other groups fronting the LaRues."

"Then the Augmented Human Rights Council—" she began.

"—Are powerless against the ones really in charge of what's going on here," he finished.

She stepped away from him. So what? They were supposed to just fight against an all-powerful force of presumably wealthy and well-connected people with no support from the military or legal counsel? She couldn't believe that he was willing to accept that.

That Morta was.

She shook her head. "We have to make it stop," she repeated. She stared at the lifeless girl again. "We can't let this happen to anyone else."

For the first time in what felt like forever, Amber wasn't just thinking about her own future. What Spade was doing was wrong. And if acquiring them would put a small dent in the death toll, she was determined to play a role in their demise.

"I will make them pay," she whispered to the girl as she stormed from the house. "I promise."

Chapter Twelve

Amber slipped into the high roller room from the secret entrance. She slid in behind a waitress carrying a tray of drinks to one of the tables. Her heart hammered in her chest uncomfortably. She didn't want to be here.

Not after what she'd seen.

But, there wasn't any other choice.

J had left her at the Underworld's entrance. One moment he'd been standing next to her, his hand resting uncomfortably on the small of her back. The next, he'd been gone. Leaving her with the strange sensation of craving his touch again.

Even now, the memory of his warmth lingered with her. She hated that he had been capable of tearing down some of her barriers. And she thought she had been so careful.

Morta was nowhere to be seen, which was normal at these types of functions. She'd make an appearance, give a grand speech about Thoth, the Underworld, and a warning for her guests to not gamble away their souls. But then she would disappear. Not even Amber knew where she went most of the time.

"No!" a man shouted at one of the blackjack tables. He slammed his fists onto the table, sending chips scattering to the ground. He stood over the female dealer, his face a mass of anger. "You cheated! I saw you do it!" he screamed.

Amber immediately felt the hair on the back of her neck lift as she stepped towards the fight. She'd witnessed this type of reaction before. Someone overextended themselves, bet something they didn't want to lose, and then lost. Classic addicts, not knowing when to quit.

The casino thanked them for their misgivings. It was how Morta had amassed much of her wealth. Today, however, it made Amber's stomach churn. How many times had one of the naturally augmented taken a risk with Spade and ended up dead because of it? She knew what Morta did was completely different than what the LaRues—and whoever was backing them—were doing, but it didn't change her sense of uneasiness.

The man gestured towards his small stack of chips. Spittle flew from his mouth as he leaned towards the dealer and snarled at her. To her credit, she didn't back down. Morta trained all her dealers on how to handle pissed off gamblers.

His hand crept towards his belt. Amber's senses screamed at her that something was wrong. Weapons weren't allowed in the Underworld, but occasionally someone was able to sneak past security with an undocumented one. Something about his movement made her think that this was one of those times.

She sighed. Maybe it was everything that had happened over the past few days. Maybe it was how tired she was after seeing the dead. Maybe it was that she was just sick of having to deal with petty people who bit off more than they could chew. But she did not have the patience for his shenanigans.

She strode towards the table confidently. Her stabilizers hummed beneath her skin as she envisioned protection for the dealer and other players. Her sole focus was on eliminating the threat to their safety.

The man leapt onto the table. He loomed over the dealer, his shoulders hunched like a bear. He swung his head up as he landed, knocking it against the chandelier hanging above the table with a loud clang. Crystals clinked together as it shuddered. The chain holding it to the ceiling groaned, dust fluttering around it.

Amber unholstered her pulser pistol in a single, fluid motion. She breathed in as she stared down the short barrel and aimed at the man. There was a loud moaning sound as the chain continued to sway. Her eyes trailed away from the man and pinpointed a bent link. It was barely connected to the one above it. An idea sparked within her and she jerked the pistol up, taking aim at the weakest link.

She pulled the trigger.

The dart struck the link just where it was beginning to break apart. It shattered into dust. The chandelier collapsed onto the table, pinning the man beneath it. Crystals exploded in a spray of shards. Holstering her pistol once more, Amber lunged for the man.

The crowd screamed as they scrambled away from the table in a panic. Amber rolled her eyes and pushed through them. Her boots crunched on glass. She tsked softly as she stared down at the man pinned beneath the weight of the giant chandelier. For a moment, she considered leaving him there. But a glance around the room told her that wasn't an option.

Pulling a magnetic cuff from one of her dress pockets, she placed it around the man's hands. He groaned as she rolled him onto his back and peered into his eyes. Dilated, unfocused pupils met her gaze. Definitely concussed. She didn't care. He deserved what he got.

Security officials stormed into the room moments later. They ushered the remaining guests away from the table. Two bulky men lifted the chandelier off the man and pulled him to his feet. He swayed unsteadily on his feet before throwing his head back in an attempt to headbutt one of them. Still sluggish from being crushed by a chandelier, his missed entirely. Another guard thrust a taser against his neck. Blue sparks sizzled as the scent of melting flesh permeated the air. Amber wrinkled her nose at the putrid scent.

The man spasmed as the current flowed through him, his hands tucking against his chest and drool sliding from his lips. When the guard finally removed the taser, the man slumped to the floor. He twitched. Once. Twice. And then lay still. The guards dragged him out of the room by his ankles.

Amber searched the crowd for the dealer. She stood in a corner. She leaned her head against the wall with her eyes closed. Her chest rose and fell in quick, staccato bursts. Her shoulders shook and Amber realized the woman was silently sobbing. Weaving her way through the remaining crowd, Amber paused right in front of the dealer.

Her mascara was running in black and silver rivers down her cheeks. Amber frowned when she noticed the way the girl scratched at the back of her hands. Deep red gashes stretched across her skin. Rivulets of crimson stained her hands. As if sensing Amber standing in front of her, her eyes snapped open and peered straight in Amber's.

Amber felt her cheeks heat. At a loss for words, she placed her hand on the woman's shoulder and squeezed.

"You alright?" she croaked.

The dealer didn't respond.

"It's over now. Why don't you go get some rest? We can handle it from here." She squeezed the woman's shoulder again. Still, there wasn't a reply.

Although a part of her felt compelled to help the dealer process the fight, the bigger, stronger part of her didn't have the emotional bandwidth to deal with another person's feelings.

Amber shrugged. "Whatever," she quipped as she turned her back on her. It wasn't her fault the dealer couldn't handle how the Underworld's guards manhandled their arrests. Or was it that she just couldn't fathom that she'd just been attacked by a player?

It didn't matter. She needed to debrief the head of security. Maybe then she could finally get some rest. She doubted it. She hated the phrase 'no rest for the wicked,' but knew it was true. In the Underworld, party never stopped.

Oliver's bald head gleamed in the overhead lights that had been turned on when the security detail arrived. Amber made her way towards him, already knowing what he was going to say.

"You should have waited for us," he said gruffly.

Amber lifted her chin to meet his gaze and smirked. "If I had waited, who knows what he might have done." She flicked her eyes toward where a set of guards was bagging the weapon the man had dropped when he'd been crushed by the chandelier. It was small and shaped like a pulser pistol with a vial attached to its top that swirled with a vibrant purple liquid.

"What is that thing, anyway?" she asked.

"Dunno," he sighed. "Never seen anything like it before. We'll be sending it off for research once Morta's given the approval."

She cocked an eyebrow at him. "No clue what he lost, but it must've been something invaluable. His dealer is rocking herself in the corner." She jerked her thumb towards the woman. "Don't know how much you'll get out of her."

"We'll get her to the medica," Oliver replied automatically. The veins in his biceps twitched as he twisted around to peer at the dealer. His jaw tightened when he saw the state she was in and motioned for two of his guards to escort her out of the room.

"Tell me what happened."

Amber made quick work of describing how she'd entered the high-roller room only a few moments before the man began verbally attacking the dealer. She described how he became physically aggressive, so she'd decided to step in. She didn't mention her "spidey-sense." No reason to spread that little tidbit of knowledge around if she didn't have to. Sure, people knew she was lucky, but she didn't want them knowing she could sense danger before it happened. Gave her an upper hand in fights.

When she'd finished, Oliver nodded once before saying, "You'd best tell Morta everything you just told me." He waved towards the door his guards had dragged the man through.

"Seriously?" she asked. Her eyes burned from exhaustion and her head ached.

The corners of his mouth twitched, but he just shook his head.

"Awesome. Wow. Gee, thanks. This is exactly how I wanted to spend my time," she sniped.

He stared at her, his eyes going wide for a moment before he cleared his throat and turned away from her.

She stood alone, in silence for a moment. Her mind raced as she silently berated herself for revealing even a modicum of her frustration to someone else. Morta's employees knew she was loyal to the Underworld—and to their employer. Yet, it would be so easy for that reputation to disintegrate into dust if rumors spread that there was a rift between her and Morta.

Her initial reaction was to follow Oliver and explain that she was just exhausted from too many days spent working overtime. Somehow, she knew it would only make it worse. Sighing heavily, she exited the room through the door the guards had taken.

The trek down the passageways to their underground holding cells made the pit in her stomach double in size. Morta had lied to her. Or, at least, she'd omitted truths about what the LaRues were using Spade for. It certainly wasn't just for gambling.

Every time Amber closed her eyes, she saw the girl's face. Her unseeing eyes. Her limp body covered in bruises and dried blood. There was something about her that reminded her how easily she could have ended up in that room.

If it hadn't been for Morta.

Even that recognition left her feeling confused. Morta had done so much for her. Beyond that, she'd expressed her desire to protect NAs. She was angry at the United Terran force for letting people like them live in constant fear of being picked up for testing. Yet, she'd withheld the fact that Spade was a front for illegal testing on NAs. She didn't know what that meant for the future. Or why the LaRues were giving up on their casino now. Her skin crawled with goosebumps and she shivered. She couldn't imagine Morta falling in with whoever was supporting the LaRues to continue the research, but still. She couldn't be sure.

Whimpering echoed down the hall, and Amber paused. Morta was already here. Biting her bottom lip, she increased her pace. Whatever was happening, she was determined for there to be no more secrets between them.

She rounded the corner, stopping short when she saw what Morta had done to the man. Thick hooks pierced the skin of his back, suspending him from the ceiling by dozens of braided wire strands. His arms hung limply by his sides, his shoulders bruised and sunken, clearly dislocated. Blood ran down his body in currents of crimson. He screamed as Morta pressed an electrifying baton into his armpit. She held it there for only a couple of seconds, but it was enough to leave him whimpering when she withdrew. The scent of melted flesh stung Amber's nostrils and she coughed as bile rose up her throat.

Morta was alone with the man. The metal walls gleamed white, making the crimson droplets splattered on them all the more jarring. Amber sucked in a breath. The carnage had never bothered her before. She didn't know why it did now.

A drain in the middle of the room sucked the crimson flood into the piping system. Tomorrow, there wouldn't be a trace of the man left. Amber already knew he'd bet his life. Not just a part of it. Not just a few years. All of it.

This is what he'd lost.

Morta never played with the ones who only stood to lose a few years of their essence. She'd told Amber once that hurting the ones who had bet everything helped her remain human. She lived the pain they experienced when she consumed their energy. Their life.

"Good," Morta said when she noticed her standing at the doorway. "I'm glad you're here."

"Why?" Amber asked before she could stop herself. She stepped into the room.

The man had obviously pissed himself. The smell of ammonia was almost overwhelming. She wrinkled her nose in distaste.

Morta peered around the man's dangling body to meet her gaze. "Because, I need your help in getting this man to tell me his name. So far, he has absolutely refused."

"I see," Amber said. She didn't want to help Morta torture him. "Couldn't you just scan his eye or something? It would be quicker. And more accurate."

"Yes, I tried that already," she replied briskly. "There was something wrong with the scan."

The man laughed, his teeth flashing red as his lips moved. "New biotech for security purposes." He coughed wetly. "You can't hack it. You can't access my files." He spat at Morta. "You really should invest in the future, Morta, instead of living in the past."

She backhanded him. A bruise blossomed on his cheek and he squirmed like a worm on a hook.

"You don't scare me," he moaned as he spat blood onto the floor.

"I should," Morta responded. "Of course, you bet your life and lost, so the only thing you have to look forward to is eternal darkness."

He laughed again. "You won't kill me," he said.

"And why not?"

"Because if you do, you'll lose any shot you have at acquiring Spade. Do you have any idea who I am?"

She shrugged. "No one of consequence. If you were, I would already know who you are."

"You're too much of a bitch to know when you've been beat. You'll never be the queen of Thoth. You'll never be able to stop the rising tide. You're just a decaying, outdated twat who is too stupid to realize that the war is already over. You lost. You—"

107

Amber didn't get to hear the rest of his speech as Morta wrapped her fingers around his throat. His eyes went wide as the transference began. They bulged from his face as his energy began to be pulled from him. Amber closed her eyes, not wanting to see his skin turn grey and begin to crumble into dust as Morta completely consumed him.

Her head was fuzzy, and she couldn't seem to pull the disparate threads she knew fit together.

The clinking of the wires drew her attention back to Morta. Her skin glistened luminously as she stalked towards her. Her lips had turned ruby red, and her dark, ebony hair shone as it caught the light. She smiled at Amber.

"Turns out, I didn't need his information after all," she said.

Amber wasn't in the mood for Morta's cockiness or swagger. The man was dead. And she had even more questions than she did before. She felt drained. Exhausted from everything that had happened. And, all she wanted to do was go back to her chambers and sleep.

"What war was he talking about, Morta?" she asked. She was too tired to care if she was pushing her luck.

Morta tucked a lock of Amber's hair behind her ear as she said, "That? It was just the ramblings of a man afraid to die. It didn't mean anything."

Amber took a step back. Clenching and unclenching her hands, she tried to stifle the anger coursing through her. Here she was again, lying to her. How many times in her life had Morta told her bold-faced lies? How many times had Amber blindly followed this woman?

"I can't believe you're still doing it!" she screamed. "I had thought—" she paused, unable to grasp the words she really wanted to say. "—I can't believe that I trusted you all these years. That I did your bidding. You're just like everyone else. You're lying to me!"

S.A. McClure

Morta held up her hands in a placating fashion. It was too little too late. Amber was already past the point of being calmed by the woman she viewed as a mother.

"You don't even have the decency to tell me the truth now, do you?" she hissed. "I saw what Spade's been doing. I saw them. The dead. Were you ever going to tell me that we were buying a front for murder in this little acquisition of yours? Do you even care that we're purchasing death along with the casinos?"

"Alright, I think there's been some sort of misunderstanding—"

"Misunderstanding!" Amber shrieked. "Are you kidding me? Come on, Morta! I know you know about the medical trials. The experiments. The dead bodies dumped into that abandoned house."

"You're right," she replied, still holding her hands up. "I do know about that."

"And you didn't tell me! You let me go into those negotiations not knowing what the LaRues have been doing to people. People like us, Morta. What in the stars!" Her voice broke as she was unable to control her emotions. She couldn't believe that Morta had been willing to be a part of this. It was the only logical reason as to why Morta hadn't told her. She wanted to continue the transactions. She wanted to feed innocent people into the research pipeline to collect what? A little cash? The idea made Amber's stomach churn.

"You betrayed me. You betrayed everything I thought we stood for!"

Morta didn't try to stop her as Amber turned from her and stormed out of the room. Hot tears streamed down her cheeks. She swiped at them angrily. What in the stars was wrong with her? She hated crying. She hated feeling this weak.

There were too many thoughts rattling around in her brain and she was too exhausted to process any of them. All she knew was that if Morta intended to feed NAs into a pipeline for illegal research, she would leave. She refused to take part in it.

109

Even if she had to make her own path again, she would do it. She'd left Earth at fifteen. She could leave now.

She didn't even bother stripping the red dress off before curling into a ball on her bed and letting sleep consume her. The last thing she saw as her mind shut off were the girl's unseeing eyes.

Chapter Thirteen

A bouquet of black roses stood on Amber's nightstand when she woke the next day. A card featuring Morta's wax seal stuck out from the blooms.

"What in the stars!" Amber groaned as she flopped over and ripped the card from its holder. She didn't know what she more disturbed by: that someone had been in her room without her knowing or that Morta had the gall to send her flowers in the first place.

Her hands shook slightly as she pulled the hand-written note from the envelop and quickly scanned its contents. Not an apology. Of course not. She had never known her employer to apologize for anything.

It was a summons.

She crumpled the paper and tossed it into the waste bin, quickly followed by the roses. She didn't like flowers anyway.

They were a waste of resources. Especially since this particular species had to be shipped in special from Earth.

Her wrist dinged as a message appeared on her bracelet. Rolling her eyes, she depressed the button on the bracelet to cast a projection of the message in front of her.

"I need to see you." Unknown transmission.

She tapped her finger on her chin as she read and reread the message. She had been anticipating a summons from Morta. This was something else. She could guess who had sent it.

J.

She couldn't think of anyone else who would contact her like this without wanting his identity known. She didn't even know his real name. Her mind immediately went to the sub-context of the message. Did he need to see her because every time he thought about her he tingled? Heat rushed to her abdomen at the thought.

She clicked respond and sent a single word in response. "When?"

She stumbled to her bathroom as she waited for him to reply. Dark streaks ran down her cheeks from where her makeup had run. Her hair was matted in some places, tangled in others, and essentially looked like a hurricane had stormed through it. She sighed. Yeah. If he could see her now, he would definitely stop thinking about her at all.

Slipping out of the dress, she took a quick shower. The hot water did little relieve the queasy feeling lingering in her stomach. She'd fallen asleep thinking of the girl and awoken to the memory of the stench of that place.

And Morta would soon be a part of it.

She couldn't forgive her.

She wouldn't.

Her bracelet dinged again. "30 minutes" with an address following.

Shutting the water off, she did a quick search for the location and discovered that he wanted to meet in a small coffee shop close to Spade's headquarters. Well, if he wanted to go to the belly of the beast, who was she to deny him?

She pulled on a black shirt and matching pants. Combat boots and her pulser pistol completed the look. As an afterthought, she slipped the NBS onto her arm before leaving. She didn't want to take any chances. Someone had already tried to kill her once. And she really didn't want to die.

Her bracelet dinged again as she entered the elevator. She didn't read it, knowing it was from Morta. Her employer was predictable, if nothing else. Amber didn't care what she had to say. Not right now. Maybe not ever again. All she knew was that she had promised that girl that she would make amends for what happened to her.

Live music echoed from the coffee shop. Synthetic sunlight had been added to all the windows, giving the place an even more whimsical feel than it already had from the decorations. Flowers grown in a greenhouse outback were at every table and fresh baked goods made Amber's mouth salivate when she entered the small shop.

She glanced around the room, expecting to see J lounging at one of the tables. From what she could see, he wasn't there. In fact, she didn't recognize a single person in the shop, which wasn't exactly a surprise, considering she didn't socialize much beyond the Underworld. But still, someone had known her direct line. She would have thought she'd know who it was.

Not wanting to be too conspicuous, she ordered a hot chocolate from the barista and took a seat at a booth in the rear corner. She leaned back and watched the door as she sipped at the hot drink. To her surprise, it tasted as if real milk had been used in it. Another rarity. She wondered how the shop stayed open if they used real goods instead of the cheaper, synthetic ones readily available on-planet.

113

Her bracelet dinged again. And, again, she ignored it. If it were the mysterious stranger trying to connect with her, they knew where she was and could find her. If it was Morta, she didn't want to see what she had to say. Not yet, anyway.

"Excuse me, miss."

Amber jumped at the voice above her and looked up to see a boy about the age of twelve standing beside her booth. How he had managed to sneak up on her without her noticing was beyond her. Maybe she really was far more distracted than she realized.

"Yes," she stammered. She took another quick sip from her mug, trying to disguise the uneasy feeling the boy gave her. Her stabilizers didn't buzz beneath her skin and her hair didn't prickle on her neck, so she doubted he was a threat. But, she couldn't be certain.

"Come with me, please," he said.

She cocked an eyebrow at him. "What for?"

"He said for you to come with me, miss. I was told I wouldn't be paid until you came."

"Of course he did," she said. The little prick didn't even have the balls to show up when expected. She rolled her eyes at the boy. "How far is it?"

He pointed at a door behind the counter. "It's just through there, miss. He said you'd be wary of going with me and to tell you that if you want everything to go smoothly with your deal that you'll meet with him."

Tilting her head at him, she pondered his words. Why would J want to discuss the negotiation between Spade and the Underworld with her? Especially in this place. It didn't make sense.

"Who sent you?" she asked.

The boy shrugged. "Don't know his name, miss. Just know that he offered to give me six hundred credits for bringing you to him. That's a whole year's worth of money in a single day."

The excitement in the boy's voice left her feeling a bit guilty that she was delaying him. Sighing heavily, she drained the remains of her drink in a single gulp. She didn't know if it was the quick drinking or the stress, but her stomach tightened as she rose and followed the boy through the door.

He led her past the shop's office and around a corner. The back rooms clearly extended farther than she had anticipated, and she couldn't help but wonder just how far the tunnels stretched. They seemed to extend on for eternity.

They turned down a series of paths that Amber couldn't track before finally coming to stop in front of a tattered and cracked metal door. An insignia had been spray painted onto it, but had long since faded into something unrecognizable.

"Good luck, miss!" the boy shouted. He bumped into her as he sprinted back the way they'd come.

She frowned after him. Weasley little ingrate. Who did he think he was leaving her like that? Well, it was too late now to do anything else other than find out who was on the other side of the door.

She rapped smartly on it. Her knuckles ached, but she ignored the fleeting discomfort.

"Hello?" she called.

Her voice echoed down the metal hallway, but no one responded.

"What in the stars?" she whispered as she rapped on the door again. She hadn't come all this way just to be ghosted on. Who even did that, anyway, other than cowards?

A loud clicking noise drew her attention. She turned just in time to see a set of piercing blue pinpricks of light illuminate the hallway. Taking a step back, she lifted her left wrist to engage the ballistic shield.

"I don't know who you are or what you want, but stay right there and I promise I won't hurt you," she called.

She reached for her pistol, only to grasp empty air.

She stilled. When was the last time she'd seen it? She knew she had it when she left her room this morning. Then she remembered that the boy had bumped into her.

"No," she whispered. She hadn't felt anything. It wasn't possible. Her abilities wouldn't fail her like that. They never had before.

Whatever was down the hall moved towards her slowly. She imagined she felt the way a mouse did when it saw a cat stalking towards it. She wasn't sure what she could do. If there was anything at all.

The shield wouldn't hold for long. Sure, she'd had it repaired following the shade's attack, but, without her pulser pistol, she didn't know how she was going to defend herself. She still had her baton, but it was a melee weapon. She would need to be close to use it, which didn't seem like the best idea.

She began to inch her way towards the coffee shop. She waited for the hum of her stabilizers to engage, but they remained silent. Tendrils of fear crept around her heart and squeezed.

"Alright then," she said, to no one in particular. She pulled the baton from its holster and increased its damage to full power. She would have fewer attacks available with that much energy coursing into it, but hopefully she wouldn't need more than a couple of strikes.

"I'm giving you one last chance," she yelled down the corridor. "Leave me alone, or else I will ensure that you won't make it out of here alive."

She hoped her attacker wouldn't pick up on her false bravado. Without her ability, she wasn't sure how strong of a fighter she really was.

The shadowy figure morphed into a humanoid shape as it sprinted towards her. It was clearly a woman, her hair tied into a long braid that swung from side-to-side as she ran towards Amber. Her eyes gleamed brilliant blue, and she carried a pulser pistol in one hand and a blade in the other. Not many people carried swords anymore. Not when there were other, more advanced weaponry available.

"What the stars!" Amber cursed as she held her shield in front of her as the woman released a spray of darts at her.

She continued moving backwards. She didn't want to turn her back on the woman for fear that she would attack her from behind. Because she thought she'd be meeting J, she hadn't worn any of her armor. She was lucky that she'd chosen to wear the ballistic shield.

"Why are you doing this?" she asked, her voice pitched.

Her bracelet dinged again. This time, Amber issued the command for the bracelet to read her messages to her.

"Amber, please come to my chambers. There is much for us to discuss."

"I'm not going to wait for you forever. Stop being a petulant child. I promise I'll explain everything when you get here."

"Honestly, I thought you were more mature than this. Perhaps I was wrong. Don't make me ask again."

"Time's up."

The last one wasn't from Morta. It was from the same, unknown number as the mysterious ones from before. *Great*, she thought, *I'm dealing with a sociopath. Just how I always wanted to die. Being tormented by someone who takes pleasure in harming others. Perfect.*

"Call Morta," she commanded her bracelet. It glowed gold before flashing her number in a holograph with the call sign.

Amber slipped an earpiece into her ear and waited as the call rang several times before clicking to voicemail.

"Seriously!" she grunted as another spray of darts struck her shield. She dialed again.

Something heavy clanked against the shield, and her entire arm reverberated from the force. Peeking her head around the edge of the shield she looked to see what had struck her. The woman had thrown the sword at her.

She was so close that Amber could see her facial features. Her expression was lax and her eyes, despite their brilliant blue light, were expressionless. It was as if the woman were little more than a robot following someone else's commands.

Trusting her instinct, Amber dashed towards the woman and jabbed the baton into her side. She flinched, clearly registering

117

the pain. Her body seized up, and she foamed at the mouth slightly before Amber pulled the baton away.

She backed up quickly, trying to put as much space between herself and the woman as possible. She wasted a split second to pick up the sword and shove it into her belt. Although she only had melee weapons, she prayed they would be enough to at least get her back to the coffee shop.

"Call Morta!" she screamed at her bracelet as the sound of the woman's feet thundered down the hallway behind her. She slammed into Amber's shield with such force that Amber stumbled backwards several steps before tripping over her own feet and falling to her butt.

More darts clanked against the shield as Amber continued to use it to guard against the woman's attack. Clearly, she had pissed off whoever was controlling her, because she was attacking much more aggressively now.

"Pick up!" she cried.

"You better have a good reason for ignoring me earlier."

She was so relieved by the sound of Morta's voice in her ear that she nearly dropped her arm. Lucky for her, she didn't because at that moment, the woman released an armor piercing dart into her shield at close range.

The shield popped several times as the metal twisted and bent from the impact. So much for the protective coating. Of course, it had absorbed so many rounds, she was surprised it had lasted this long.

"What was that?" Morta demanded.

"I'm in trouble."

"I can hear that. Where are you?"

Amber grunted as the shield began to heat as the woman released another spray of stun darts into the damaged shield. She flexed her fingers as the hair was singed off her knuckles.

"If I don't make it back, I'm sorry I avoided you," she said. She meant it, too. Despite how angry she was, Morta had always been there for her.

"What do you mean, 'if I don't make it back?'" Morta hissed.

"I'm sorry," Amber said. "I truly—"

The line went dead.

"Void!" Amber cursed.

She clicked the button to withdraw the shield into itself. It crackled as it forced itself to fold up and retract. At least it wouldn't be in the way. Her baton hummed beneath her fingers as she brandished it at the woman.

She fired, and Amber ducked. She didn't know how she avoided the darts. Pure dumb luck, if she had to guess, since her stabilizers still weren't humming with the onslaught of her power.

She lunged for the woman, who sidestepped her. It seemed like such an effortless motion that Amber wondered just how modified this woman was. Her eyes were clearly bio-enhanced, but she also seemed to sense movements just a shade quicker than the average person.

Amber didn't really have time to think about it as the woman pointed the pulser pistol straight at her head. Red light glowed from the darts ready to explode from it.

Cursing, Amber swiped her baton at the woman and somehow managed to connect with her hand. The pistol steamed as the electrified baton met with its barrel. The woman didn't seem to notice the melting metal as she dropped the weapon. Instead, she simply reached into her belt and drew her own baton.

Wonderful, Amber thought as their weapons clanked off of one another. *Just what I always dreamed about. A melee fight with a crazy murderer.*

They remained locked together. Amber's muscles strained as she tried to gain the advantage. Her arms quivered, but couldn't force the woman down. Ways to escape zipped through her mind, but nothing seemed plausible. Her hands ached from holding the baton so tightly. Soon enough, the woman would be able to disarm—and, if so inclined—kill her.

"Who sent you?" she asked.

The woman's face didn't change. It was if she hadn't even heard Amber's question, which she knew couldn't be the case.

"Please, don't do this," she said. "We can work something out. Whatever they've offered you, I can double it."

What she meant was that Morta could double it. Not even the bribe seemed to register with the woman.

"Okay then. Fine. I can tell that we're at an impasse. You want it that way, you've got it."

Amber shuddered as she breathed in deeply. Using what strength she had left, she shoved her baton against the woman. Her feet slid across the floor as she continued to push. Just as her arms gave out, she ducked low and knocked the baton into the woman's knees. She stumbled and fell. Amber scrambled away. She turned left and then right, not knowing if she were going in the correct direction at all. For all she knew, she could be heading straight for another trap.

But it didn't matter. She just knew she needed to put as much space between her and the crazy, killer woman as possible.

She slammed her hand into keypads as she went, hoping one of them would be unlocked. Each time, they flashed red and released a shrill "beep." Sweat dripped from her brow. She kept glancing behind her, expecting to see the woman there at any moment.

Her smashed her palm into another reader. It scanned her slowly, the faint white light moving from the top to the bottom of the screen as she waited. She hopped from one foot to the other anxiously. To her relief, the pad flashed green and the door began to slide backwards.

She took the time to depress the button on her baton and wait for the charge to build at its end. It sizzled and popped when she finally plunged it into the scanner.

"Suck it," she growled as she glanced behind her one last time. She ducked into the room and slammed the door shut behind her. To her surprise, there was a deadbolt screwed into the door, which she shoved into place.

The woman pounded on the door. It rattled, but the lock held. The room was dimly lit, and Amber had to squint to see anything. She searched for additional weapons, but all she found were musty, decaying clothes, a few papers covering the lone table in the room, and a dead tablet. She checked her bracelet, but the screen had been shattered during one of the blasts from the pulser pistol. She couldn't call Morta back.

Frustrated, she leaned her head back against the door and sank to the ground. If Morta couldn't find her, she'd die in this hell hole. She was sure of it. She had no food. No water. No additional weapons. Her shield was basically useless. She examined her baton. Its battery indicator was less than fifty percent, which meant it would die sometime over the next three hours, depending on how much of a charge she let it build before using it.

If she even survived that long.

Shaking her hands out, she focused on finding the core of her abilities. Her brow furrowed as she concentrated. She expected her stabilizers to hum beneath her skin. Nothing happened. Throwing her hands up, she dropped her head back into the wall and slid to the ground.

She was trapped.

She didn't know if anyone was coming.

She would most likely die.

Alone.

In a musty, old room in the middle of Thoth's underground tunnels.

Laughter bubbled in her stomach and she couldn't contain herself as she released it.

So much for being the luckiest woman alive.

An explosion on the other side of the door shook Amber to her bones. Covering her head with her hands, she ducked as shrapnel from the door exploded inwards. Steam clouded the room, making it difficult for her to see past the molten metal flowing to the floor from a hole in the door.

Spade

Metal shards sliced her palms open as she crawled across the floor. She scrambled behind a table.

This was it. This was the end.

Chapter Fourteen

Crouching behind a table, Amber clenched her baton in her hand. Blood flowed freely from the cuts on her palms, making her grip slick. She snarled. Lucky or not, she didn't want to die cowering behind a table. She wanted to die fighting.

She leapt to her feet and approached the door slowly. She held the baton at her side, its tip crackled as she waited for the charge to build up.

The sound of punches and breaking flesh filtered through the dull ringing in her ears. She blinked several times, trying to clear her mind.

"Hello?" she called. Her voice sounded feeble, even to her own ears.

Something gurgled beyond the door. Amber stumbled backwards a step. She breathed in slowly, trying to calm the pounding of her heart in her ears.

"Are you alright?" a masculine voice called through the hole in the door.

Amber froze as recognition hit her.

"Frost?" she asked.

"Yeah," he answered. "What are you doing down here?"

She was so relieved to hear someone she knew that she didn't pause to ask why he was down there. All she wanted was out.

"Meeting with a friend," she called. He chuckled at her, and she wondered if he knew more than he was letting on. Her hand trembled as she slid the deadbolt back and cracked the door open.

"Let's get you out of there, then," he said. He smiled down at her.

"Where's the woman?" she asked, flicking her eyes from side to side, trying to determine where she had gone.

"She won't be a problem anymore. I promise. Just come out."

She peeked her head out the door and glanced up and down the hallway. The woman was slumped on the floor, blood trickling from the corner of her mouth. She looked away quickly. She had seen too much death over the past twenty-four hours. She didn't want or need to see more.

"You're alright, now," Frost soothingly. "Just come out."

Numbness crept through her. She couldn't process what he was saying or what she was seeing.

Warm hands clamped around her wrists, tugging her through the door. He enveloped her in a tight embrace. He smelled of sweat and oil and blood.

He cradled her head in his hands and whispered in her ear, "It's going to be alright. Shh."

Even as he held her, discomfort writhed within her. She didn't like being touched, especially by people she didn't trust. And she didn't trust him. He'd given her no reason to.

Her hands dropped to her sides and she stepped backwards. His grip tightened for a moment, as if he were going to refuse letting her go. But then he relaxed his hold on her.

"I need to go home," she whispered, refusing to look at the dead woman.

"Ok," he said. He reached over and tucked a lock of her hair behind her ear.

She flinched away from him. His jaw muscles twitched, but he didn't say anything as he motioned for her to follow him.

"What about the woman?" she asked.

"What about her?"

Amber faltered. His tone was cold and harsh, the way it had been in the negotiations.

"How did you know I was down here?" she inquired, changing the subject.

"Honestly, I didn't know it was you. We have motion sensors down here, so we knew someone was here." He turned to face her. "Why were you down here?"

She shrugged. She couldn't tell if he were lying or not, but if he were, then she didn't want to reveal to him that she couldn't use her abilities right now. She wasn't sure why she still couldn't sense whether he was a danger to her or not. But then, he had saved her, hadn't he?

Sighing, she decided to tell him the truth. At least, a partial truth. "I really was supposed to be meeting someone. One of the waiters in the café told me to come down here."

He jerked his head towards her at that admission. "What waiter?" he asked.

"I don't know," she said. "A boy. Couldn't have been older than maybe twelve."

He turned on her, blocking her path down the hall. "You mean to tell me that you actually decided to follow a boy into the tunnels? How arrogant are you?" He rubbed his chin as he spoke. Shadows shrouded his face so she couldn't see his eyes.

"I thought—"

"Stars!" he cursed, cutting her off. "You do realize you almost died down here, right? Do you have any idea what she was?"

125

Amber shook her head. The movement made her dizzy, and she wished she could sit down and sleep. She didn't understand why her body was refusing to cooperate.

"I'm sorry," she whispered. She didn't know what else to say. She didn't know why he cared so much. They were enemies, after all.

He ran his hand through this hair, tousling it. "Fortuna, you are one of the most interesting women I've ever met, but you are also so infuriating. Do you always run headlong into danger without considering the consequences?"

She smirked at him. "Hazard of always having things work out for me," she said.

He stared at her for several seconds, continuing to block her path. She sensed that he wanted to say something more, but didn't want to ask what it was. Eventually, he sighed and turned his back on her without saying anything at all.

They continued in silence, with only the sound of their footfalls interrupting her thoughts.

Beams of light illuminated the hallway in front of them as a dozen men, all bearing the Underworld's insignia formed a barrier in front of them. Frost glanced back at her, a questioning look on his face.

"I called Morta," she answered.

He gave her a lopsided smile before pressing his back against the wall and waving them towards her. "She's all yours, gents."

"I have never, in all my years of working with you, been this disappointed, Amber," Morta said as she sipped from her glass of wine. They were alone in her office. "What were you thinking!"

Amber shrank away from Morta in her seat. She didn't want to be scolded. She was an adult, not a child, and she didn't appreciate Morta constantly making her feel like she wasn't capable of handling herself.

"I thought J was the one who messaged me," she said. She didn't know for certain that he hadn't been the one to message her. She didn't know how to contact him, so she didn't even have a way to ask.

"And you just thought, what, that it would be a good idea to go investigate on your own? Without letting anymore know where you were going? You could have died down there!"

"I know," she whispered. She recoiled further into the chair's cushions. "I'm sorry, Morta. I don't know what to tell you."

Morta snarled and looked away from her. "I don't know who you are anymore."

Her words were like a lash against Amber's heart. Even now, after everything she'd found out about Morta, she didn't want her to be disappointed in her. What was wrong with her? She didn't want to constantly seek her approval. She didn't want to feel as small as she did right now.

Her anxiety morphed into anger. "You're one to talk!" she yelled.

Morta raised an eyebrow at her and opened her mouth to respond. The unsettled argument from the night before bubbled within Amber, feeding her anger.

She leapt to her feet. "You wanna know why I didn't tell you where I was going or why I thought it was J? Because I don't trust you. How can I? You knowingly chose to acquire Spade, even though they engage in illegal experiments. What were you planning on doing? Continuing them as you grow your empire? I don't want any part of that!"

She panted, her heart beating erratically in her chest as her anger died as quickly as it had sprung to life. Her shoulders shook as she glared at Morta, daring her to refute what she already knew.

Morta released a long, slow breath and tapped her nails on her desk. "Is that what you honestly think about me?" she asked. She didn't sound angry. Or frustrated. Just sad.

That wasn't the reaction Amber had been anticipating. "Yes," she responded defiantly. Even if a shred of doubt was creeping into the recesses of her mind.

"I see."

Amber gaped at her. Where was the righteous fury? Or, at the very least, the adamant denial? She didn't know how to process this response.

"I need time to process," she said. "I need space."

"Okay."

Again, Amber didn't know how to respond to Morta. She'd never known the woman to be at a loss for words. She met her gaze, but found only stoic hardness reflecting back at her.

"Thank you," she said.

Morta cleared her throat. "The paperwork came through," she said. "The acquisition is complete. All you have to do is meet with their delegation one last time to pick up the hard copies. I already have the soft ones."

She stood there for several seconds processing the fact that Morta still wanted her to facilitate the closing of the deal.

"You can't be serious," she said.

Morta shrugged. "They already know and trust you. It makes sense for you to finish this."

"And if I refuse?"

"Then you refuse, and I will not force you."

She considered. Her stabilizers still weren't working properly, so she wasn't sure if this was a trap or not. In all honesty, she didn't know what to think. She didn't want to believe that Morta condoned the testing or the death. But then, she hadn't denied it either.

"Do you know who's trying to kill me?" she asked.

"No," Morta responded. "Honestly, Amber. If I did, I wouldn't rest until they had been squashed from this world like the cockroach they are."

"Oh."

"I know you don't believe anything I'm saying right now, but I need you to know that I am only doing the best that I can."

Amber cocked an eyebrow. Was that a hint of vulnerability in Morta's voice or was she hallucinating? She breathed in deeply to give herself time to process. She didn't want to tell her about her lack of power. Not until she had figured out what had happened to her, anyway.

"When do you want me to meet with them?" she asked as she sank back into the chair. She didn't trust herself to stand right now.

A smile tugged at the corners of Morta's lips. "The plan was to send you this afternoon. I want this finalized as soon as possible."

"So that you can turn into the monster killing innocent kids?" She couldn't stop herself, but she regretted the words as soon as they were out.

Morta's face remained impassive as she said, "I am shocked this is what you think of me. But, I suppose I should have been more honest with you from the start."

"Yeah, you think?"

Morta tapped her fingers on the desk again, her eyes drilling into Amber's. "I recognize that there is much for us to discuss, Amber. But we don't have time to hash out all the gritty little details right now."

"That's what you always say," she responded petulantly.

"I know. And I'm sorry."

Amber crossed her arms over her chest and waited for Morta to continue. When she didn't, she said, "Your secrets are going to be your destruction."

Morta chuckled at that. "Yes, they probably will be." She paused, her eyes searching Amber's face. "I need you to do this for me. I know you're struggling to trust me right now, and that's on me. I should have been more forthcoming about the reasons why I want to acquire Spade. I'm sorry I didn't tell you more sooner. And I'm sorry we don't have time for me to tell you now. But I need you to trust me."

Amber sat on the chair as still as a statue as she contemplated Morta's words. Her body ached, and her mind was fuzzy. She still couldn't engage her stabilizers, no matter how much she tried.

Balling her hands into fists, she said, "Fine. But I have a few conditions."

Morta motioned for her to proceed, and she did.

"First, I want an additional person to join us for the final meeting. All we need is the signed paperwork. I mean it's already official, right, so this is more of a symbolic meeting anyway. Second, I need a few hours to rest. I almost died—again—today, and I can't go back out there until I've had some time to decompress. Capeesh?"

"I think I can arrange both of your requests."

"Good," Amber said as she rose from the chair. "Now, if you'll excuse me, I'm going to go take a nap."

The door was just sliding open when Morta called after her, "I'm glad you're safe, Fortuna. We need you here. More than you know."

She hesitated at the door. Morta rarely said things like that to her or anyone else. For a moment, the bands tightening around her heart loosened as she envisioned turning back to her and telling her that she knew she couldn't possibly want to be involved with the shady enterprise of experimenting on NAs. But then she remembered the girl's unseeing eyes and the stench of the room. She remembered how focused Morta had been on procuring Spade for herself.

Gritting her teeth, she shook her head and strode from the room. She didn't know if she imagined it or not, but she thought she heard Morta sigh as the doors slid shut.

Chapter Fifteen

Amber twiddled her thumbs as she lounged on the chaise. A fire roared in the hearth. The sack of incense she'd placed in it cast a warm, vanilla and citrus scent around the room. She glanced at her bracelet for the fourth time in under ten minutes.

The Spade delegation was already over an hour late to the meeting.

She shared a glance with Jasper. He didn't need to speak or say a word for her to know what he was thinking. The deal had gone sour; it just hadn't been confirmed yet.

"How much longer do we have to wait?" Bella asked from where she stood by the fire. She was a relatively new addition to the Underworld's family of NAs, and Amber still wasn't sure what her power was. She had been surprised when Morta assigned the younger girl to accompany them. But, she wasn't in a place to argue with her employer.

"We will wait until Morta signals for us to return home. Until then, make yourself comfortable," Amber replied, her tone unusually harsh. She regretted how unkind her words sounded the moment they left her.

"But what if they never come, and Morta never calls us home?" Bella pressed.

Amber rolled her eyes at Jasper as they shared another glance. This was supposed to be a symbolic meeting to close the deal. The paperwork had already been signed and delivered electronically. But, Morta was old-fashioned and wanted the hard copies delivered to her as well.

Still, the wait made Amber's insides flutter as she imagined all the things that could have gone wrong. She'd seen Frost only a few hours before, when he'd saved her from...whatever that woman had been. But they hadn't had time to discuss why he was there or what had happened. Every time she thought about what would have happened if he hadn't been there, she felt as if she were going to vomit.

She needed a distraction.

"So, Bella, tell us more about your powers."

Bella's cheeks turned a strange shade of orange, and her nose crinkled.

"Morta told me not to tell you until it was absolutely necessary."

"And do you always do everything she tells you to?" Amber asked, cocking an eyebrow at the girl. "How old are you anyway?"

She didn't look a day over fifteen, but Amber doubted the girl was that young. Then again, she reminded herself, she had only been sixteen when she landed on Thoth and needed someone to take her in. Morta had been there for her every day since then.

"I'm seventeen in three days."

"So young," Amber replied. Her throat caught as memories crept into the recesses of her mind.

"My parents worked on one of the mining moons orbiting Thoth," Bella resumed. Her voice cracked a bit when she mentioned them, but she continued on as if nothing had happened. "They died in a mining accident when I was seven."

Amber stared at the girl. She was short but sturdily built with long, auburn hair which grazed the small of her back when it wasn't pulled into a bun at the nape of her neck. A small diamond chip sparkled in her nose and eyebrow. She wore a bracelet ring over her left hand. Its dark metal glistened as the miniscule jewels embedded in it reflected the firelight. She exuded confidence and strength. But, when Amber looked close enough, she could see the sadness lingering in the girl's eyes.

"I'm sorry," she said after a moment's pause. She knew what it was to lose both parents without control. Without being able to save them. She knew what it was to be alone in a world that didn't care.

"Eh, it was a long time ago. I'm more worried about whether or not the Spade delegation is coming or not."

Classic move. Amber had to give the girl props. Seamless deflection took years to cultivate. Before she could say as much, the sound of footsteps squelching in muck and water interrupted their conversation. Amber turned towards the door just in time to see not just the three members of Spade from before, but also someone new.

Frost looked passively at her, as if he hadn't just saved her life hours before. He didn't meet her gaze as the three returning members formed a line and waited for the newcomer to advance.

Her jaw dropped open as she realized that the plump, short man with balding hair and hard, cold eyes was none other than Laurie LaRue. He was only outranked by the head of the family, Justine.

He pointed a finger directly at Amber, his jowls jiggled as he yelled, "You have my son, and I want him back!"

Amber blinked. Her hair stood on end as she grasped for a way to calm the man standing before her. An ember of heat sank into her belly, slowly swelling as the stabilizers embedded in her forearms began to hum softly. Relief coursed through her as she slowly raised her hands in the air and took a step towards him. He glared at her, his teeth bared.

"I'm sure that if we all just take a seat at the table that we'll be able to figure out a solution to this——"

"Are you slow or just stupid?" he asked as he strode towards her. Spittle coated his chin, making him look like a pig out to eat. "Your bitch of an employer stole my son. I want him back. I don't care what you have to do. But he WILL be returned to me." He jabbed his finger into her chest.

Heat coursed through her veins at his touch. She flinched. Gritting her teeth to stop herself from springing upon him, she took a small step back.

"Ok. So, let me get this straight. You think that Morta would actually steal your son in the middle of a negotiation to acquire your gambling syndicate?" She chuckled at her own words. "I should ask you the same thing. Are you slow or just stupid?" Amber knew she was being reckless, but did not like being accused of something that never happened.

Laurie's cheeks turned a vibrant red. He sputtered, clearly not used to being talked to in this manner.

Amber's stabilizers buzzed beneath her skin, sending a spike of warmth up her arms as she stared him down. She would have to figure out why they'd failed her earlier. But for now, she was thankful that her abilities were back in action.

From the corner of her eye, she saw Guinevere step forward. Laurie held up a hand, and the girl stilled.

"I know you have my son. He attended your little party last night. Stars knows how much he bet to have caused your employer to take him. I don't care what the debt is. I want him back."

Amber glanced at Jasper, who shrugged. She could only think of one person who had been taken to a holding cell last night.

Unfortunately, there was no chance that he could ever be returned to the LaRues. He was dead.

She closed her eyes and breathed out slowly. Her body still ached from everything she'd been through over the past week. She swore she still had bruises from the shade's attack that were now hurting anew because of the crazy woman from the tunnels.

"You're sure your son played in the Underworld last night?" she asked. She prayed there was a chance that the man Morta had killed hadn't been a member of the LaRue family. There was a chance he had left the casino with someone. Or crashed at a friend's house. Just because he hadn't come home yet didn't mean he'd been the man Morta had killed.

"He was there," Laurie said.

Clenching her hands tightly, Amber gave herself a moment to panic before asking, "Do you have a picture of him? There was only one person last night who ended up in our holding cell. I'd like to verify that it was him."

He jerked his head towards Frost, who stepped forward with a holographic cube. He depressed a button on the top and beams of light shot out, producing a 3D model of who Amber presumed was Laurie's son.

The minute she saw his beady, too narrow eyes, she knew it was the same man she'd arrested last night. Her heart skipped a beat as she stared at the holograph.

She contemplated lying. She didn't owe this man anything. Not anymore. The meeting was symbolic. The deal was already done, and there was nothing they could do about it. She didn't need to bring more trouble to the Underworld.

But, as she stared at the trembling man before her, she knew that would be the coward's way out. All this man wanted was answers. He wanted the power to make things right again. She knew exactly how that felt. Setting her jaw, she made her decision.

"Your son made a bad bet last night at the Blackjack table."

The man snorted. "And that's a reason to imprison him?"

She sighed, knowing her next words were likely to cause a fight. She moved her hands behind her back and signaled to Jasper to be ready. She hoped he understood her quick signing. Morta had made all of them learn a few, key phrases in hand language for these precise moments.

"I'm sure you've heard the rumors. The Underworld's motto is 'be careful not to gamble away your soul,' and we mean it."

"Just give him back to me, and this can all go away," Laurie sputtered.

Amber was surprised he hadn't realized where this conversation was going yet. She stole a glance at Frost, whose face had become ashen. He clearly had.

"I'm afraid there's nothing to give back. Your son bet the entirety of his life last night," she sucked in a deep breath, knowing the man would, most likely, attack her. "He might have been able to plead for his life successfully, except that he accused one of our dealers of cheating. He threatened her and the rest of the players at his table. I'm sorry—"

"You little bitch!" Laurie screamed as he pulled a pulser pistol from his belt and aimed it directly at Amber's head.

Great, she thought as her eyes darted around the room, searching for anything that could help her get out of this fiasco.

She continued to hold up her hands as she said in the most pacifying tone she could, "I don't want to hurt you. But I will if it means protecting my people. Their safety is the only that matters to me right now."

His finger tightened on the trigger. Her stabilizers hummed beneath her skin as she tried to assess what to do next. She wasn't certain they could survive a four on three match. Her powers, while useful, had just returned, and she was certain Guinevere would do anything she could to stop Amber from influencing the fight.

"Just tell me where my son is," Laurie demanded.

She breathed in deeply. It was now or never. "He's dead."

The words hung in the air as silence filled the room. For a moment, she thought the news had shocked him enough to debilitate him. But then, as if in slow motion she saw his arm jerk as he pulled the trigger.

The high-velocity dart zipped through the air at the same time a wall of ice formed in front of her face. The ice shattered into thousands of shards as the dart exploded before her. She blinked, too stunned by the realization that Frost had just saved her life to react.

She breathed in and out, her heart pounding. Her stabilizers burned beneath her skin as her body's natural defenses took hold. She collapsed to the floor just as three more darts shot at her in quick succession, narrowly missing her.

Retrieving the replacement pistol she'd taken from Morta's armory, she selected the darts meant to stun her opponents and released a spray of them at Guinevere and Sparrow.

A loud grunt let her know she'd struck at least one of them. Her bet was on Sparrow, since he didn't have the ability to manipulate quantum probability. Rolling to the side, she ducked beneath the table and aimed at Laurie. She released another spray of darts. Three of them struck him in the leg, sending him reeling to the ground.

Two down, two to go. Or was it one? She scanned the room to find Frost and Bella locked in a fight. Jasper was nowhere to be seen. She could only hope that he'd managed to slip from the room and call for help.

Movement at her side drew her attention just as Guinevere threw a punch at her jaw. The impact sent her head lolling to the side. Disoriented, Amber swung haphazardly around the room. By pure dumb luck, she managed to make a connection.

Her knuckles ached as she withdrew her hand. She discharged a dart in the same direction as her hit. There was a sizzling sound as it struck its target at close range. Guinevere slumped on the ground, a bruise covering one cheek. She twitched slightly when Amber poked her. Her chest rose and fell, so she wasn't dead.

Amber didn't hesitate. There was only one left.

She looked up in time to see Bella hit Frost with a ball of purple flame. It glittered as it melted away an ice shield he'd formed around himself.

Although she was still dizzy from Guinevere's hit, Amber rushed forward and placed herself between Frost and Bella.

"Wait!" she screamed, throwing her hands up. "Bella, he saved my life. You have to give him a chance to explain."

Bella looked between the two of them, her eyes widening and a frown cresting her lips.

"You and him?" she asked, her voice full of disbelief. "You would betray her like that?"

She didn't have to say her name for Amber to know the girl meant Morta.

"It's not like that," she stammered. Her cheeks were on fire and she knew that if she were looking in the mirror they would be crimson. "I swear."

Bella took a step backwards. "How can I believe you?" she asked. "He saved your life for what? Because he cares for you with unrequited love? How romantic," she spat the last word like it was disgusting to even consider.

Amber was getting really sick and tired of people assuming things about her that weren't true. What did this girl even know about her, other than that she had idealized her for years?

"Look, kid, I didn't ask for any of this. Trust me when I say that I don't want us to fight. Okay? He saved my life," she paused, "twice now. In a single day. The least I owe him is a chance to explain himself."

A ball of flame formed between Bella's fingers. The hair on the back of Amber's neck soared as she regarded the girl. Of course Morta would send an excessively loyal, though rather lunatic-worthy, minion to help with this deal.

"Bella," she warned as she pointed her pistol at the girl.

"Which do you think is faster? Your dart or my fireball?"

"I would rather not test that question," Amber admitted. "Listen, I'll drop my pistol if you diminish your flame. Is that a deal?"

They stared at each other for several moments. Without Guinevere to intervene, Amber was confident she would be able to evade the fireball. Her natural abilities would kick in and save her the way they always had. Either that or Frost would save her again. She forced herself not to look at him, instead remaining solely focused on Bella.

Slowly, the purple flames began to weaken. Amber lowered her arm and clicked the safety back into place on her pistol as the last of the fire disappeared entirely. She breathed a sigh of relief.

"This doesn't mean I won't char you in the future," Bella hissed.

"I wouldn't have it any other way."

A smile crept along Amber's lips. She saw so much of herself in this girl, it wasn't even funny. She wondered if this was the reason Morta had chosen Bella to accompany her and Jasper to the final meeting.

Frost cleared his throat behind her, and she turned to meet his gaze. He smiled sheepishly at her. "Thanks for saving me," he said.

She shrugged. "It was nothing."

He closed the gap between them and placed his hands on her shoulders. "No, it wasn't. Don't say that." He pulled her into an embrace for the second time that day. Her stomach cramped at the hug.

She still didn't like being touched.

Gently, she shoved against his chest to create space between them. "I didn't get to say it earlier. Thank you for saving my life. Twice now."

"Consider us almost even," he joked.

She rolled her eyes at him. "Sure."

"Gross," Bella said. "Get a room or something, why don't you."

Amber spun around to glare at her, but Bella had already turned her back on them and was crouched over Guinevere. Amber assumed she was checking for a pulse.

"Do you have the physical papers?" she asked, turning her attention back to Frost.

He shook his head.

Amber swept her arm across the room. "How are you going to explain this to Justine?"

He shrugged.

"Are you going to answer me? I think this is kind of an important thing."

His blue eye glowed slightly as he lifted his chin to meet her eyes. "This can only mean one thing, Amber. War. Between our syndicates."

She shook her head, not wanting to believe what she already knew. She'd known it the moment she'd seen that man's face glowing in the hologram. Morta had killed one of the LaRue family members and would have to pay for it.

"We can stop it," she began. "We can explain—"

"—explain what? That your master is a cold-hearted bitch who kills for pleasure? She's a sociopath, Fortuna."

She slapped him even before she knew what she was doing. "How dare you!" she snapped. "You don't even know her!"

"I know enough! She didn't have to kill him. But she chose to anyway."

His words gave her pause. Morta was a killer. But she also showed mercy, when mercy was due.

"Tell Justine that the deal is still on, with or without the physical copies. We already have the digital versions, as do our lawyers. There's no way she reclaim her casinos now. It would be best for everyone if the LaRues left Thoth and never returned."

He shook his head at her. "If you really think they'll accept his murder without penance, then you're a fool."

"I can't change what happened, Frost," she shrugged. "But I can offer you a chance to be on the winning side. You saved my life. I know I'll be able to petition Morta to let you stay with us."

"As if I would ever align with that"—he glowered at her—"abomination."

Amber scowled at him. Morta was many things, but she was not an object of disgust.

"Fine. Then you'll die with the rest of them if any member of the LaRue family attacks us again. I will ask Morta to forgive this transgression, since it was clear Laurie was under high distress. But, let me be very clear, Frost. If he attacks again, there won't be a next time."

He smirked at her, an infuriating gleam in his eye. "I'm sure the LaRues will be delighted to hear that they finally have an excuse to put Morta in her place."

Amber hesitated for a moment, hoping Frost would change his mind. When he didn't, she motioned for Bella to follow her from the room.

"For what it's worth," she said, as she passed him, "I hope I never see you again."

Chapter Sixteen

Sirens blasted and lights flashed brilliant white, pulling Amber from her slumber. Groggily, she pressed a button on her bracelet, and a holographic image burst to life in front of her.

"Warning. Unidentified intruders detected. Warning. Warning."

The phrase continued to repeat. Lumbering from her bed, Amber wrapped a silk kimono around her shoulders and sent a quick message to Morta asking what was going on. When no response came, she pulled on a pair of boots and exited her room.

Red lights flashed, disorienting her as she ambled down the hallway. Half-dead to the world, she bumped into people as they ran in the opposite direction she was heading. They whispered about the blood. So much blood. And death. Her mind couldn't wrap itself around their words.

She placed a hand against the cold metal of the wall, letting it awaken her just a smidge. The voice from the holograph blared all around her, calmly requesting that everyone take refuge.

Ignoring the command, she raced towards the cacophony of screams.

She slipped on the metal floor, her feet sliding out in front of her. She grasped the handrail to keep herself from falling. Thick, still warm liquid coated her feet. It took her a second to realize that it was blood. Crimson stained the walls and was smeared across the floor. Her stomach somersaulted at the sight of it. There was so much—too much—of it.

Not just the hair on her neck rose as she shot around a corner. She'd forgotten her pulser pistol and baton in her room. Stars! She hated her limited capacity to remember things.

Bodies smoldered where they'd been struck down by explosive darts. Gaping holes covered their chest cavities. Some didn't have heads. Others had flesh so charred they were barely recognizable as human. Her skin crawled at the sight. It didn't matter who these people were. They didn't deserve to die like this.

She prayed Morta hadn't been on the main floor of the casino when—whatever this was—began. Sure, she was angry at her, but she didn't want her to die. She didn't want to lose another person who meant something to her.

She lost count of the bodies. Shoving aside the smell of burnt flesh and the shit spray, Amber charged into the main floor of the casino. Every single security guard was pressed into a tight circle. It could only mean one thing: Morta was here.

Several of them pointed their pistols at her as she approached, hands high in the air.

"It's me," she called. None of them responded. "Please, Morta. Tell them to let me through."

One of the guards stepped forward slightly. "Fortuna?" he asked.

"Yes, it's me!" she sighed in relief. She didn't know why the rest of them didn't recognize her. She thought she'd known all the guards employed in the Underworld, but their faces didn't look familiar.

"She's been badly wounded. We were ordered to wait here until the medic arrived," the guard was saying, drawing her attention back to him.

"What do you mean she's been 'badly wounded?'" Amber asked. Sweat soaked the small of her back as the image of Morta lying on a table before being incinerated and shot into space filled her mind. The girl's unseeing dead eyes followed in quick succession. Her brow furrowed and her eyes stung.

Shaking her head, she leaned towards the man and said in a conspiratorial voice, "If you let me see her, I will owe you a favor." She winked at him for good measure.

To her surprise, he rolled her eyes at her. "I know your tricks, Fortuna. I've seen you in action one too many times. Look, if it were up to me, which it's not, I would let you through to see her. But I'm not. And you're not the medic. So, I'm going to have to ask you to take your manipulative ways away from here."

For a second, Amber just stared at the man, her mouth gaping open. And then, anger struck her. "First of all, Mr. Rude, I'm here because these blasted sirens went off. Second of all, Morta would trust me to be by her side if she were mortally wounded. You're making me think she is, therefore, you will let me pass."

They stared at each other for a moment. Amber crossed her arms over her chest and scowled at him.

The guard opened and shut his mouth several times before finally saying, in his most appreciative voice, "I know you're only trying to do what's best for her. I get it. But having you here, when she's in her weakened state, is something she will not forgive lightly. You know leaving is the best thing to do right now."

"I don't know that, actually, but thank you for making me doubt myself. Look. I just want to know she's okay. And I honestly won't believe anyone but her. So, you don't have any other choice but to let me pass."

"Let her through," Morta's strained voice said through the rows of guards. "Let me see her." She coughed.

Amber shot the guard a look of 'I told you so' before slipping past him. Morta's left eye was completely swollen shut, and a mixture of puss and blood was seeping from a cut on her eyebrow. Dark purple splotches ran across her face like craters on a moon. Muscle pulsed beneath the thin layer of torn skin covering her wounds.

"What happened?" Amber gasped as she dropped to her knees before her.

Morta shuddered as she lifted her chin and met Amber's gaze. "Clearly, we were attacked."

"Yes, but by who? And why?"

Wheezing, Morta lifted a slip of paper from the floor. Droplets of red dripped from its corner as she shoved it into Amber's hand. "Read it," she murmured.

Amber grasped the paper, her fingers trembling. A part of her already knew what it would say. They had killed Justine LaRue's nephew. Well, to be fair, Morta had been the one to do it. She had made that choice. And the entirety of the Underworld was being punished for her mistakes.

She scanned the tight, cursive scrawl, and her heart sank. They were the legal owners of Spade, but the LaRues would never be satisfied. Not now. They vowed they wouldn't stop launching attacks—bloodbaths—on the casino until Morta experienced a loss the way they had.

A life for a life.

Amber crumpled the paper in her fist and glared at Morta. "You did this," she hissed. "You just couldn't resist consuming all of what that man bet, could you."

"You know I warn everyone who enters here to be careful not to gamble away their soul."

"Yes! I do know that! But did you ever stop to consider most of our guests don't realize that you're actually serious about sucking the life out of them?"

Morta coughed again, and a bubble of blood blossomed on her lips. Amber stopped yelling at her, concern overtaking her every thought. She was angry. She was disappointed. She was drained. But mostly, she just wanted things to get better.

"You are still very young, Fortuna. You don't understand. Not yet."

She shot to her feet and turned away from her. That was the last nail in the coffin, as far as Amber was concerned. She closed her eyes, the dead girl stared back at her. Clenching her hands tightly, she released a long, slow breath. "I will stay until the deal is officially finalized. After that, I don't know."

Morta didn't try to stop her as she stormed away. The death toll was rising. And Amber was running out of time to stop it.

Amber paced back-and-forth in Morta's office as she waited for the other woman to arrive. She didn't know why she was here. Why she had accepted Morta's invitation to discuss what had happened that morning. The death. The lies.

The future.

Nervously, she fumbled with her bracelet. She kept checking and re-checking for messages. She hadn't received anything from the mysterious messenger. Although she'd initially believed it was J, now she wasn't so sure. Full of nervous energy, she paced back and forth across the room.

The office's door hissed as it slid open, and Morta strode in. Her wounds were almost completely healed. Amber wasn't surprised. She had a long list of people who 'owed' her years of their life. And, each time Morta consumed their energy, she grew not only younger, but also stronger.

"I am so thankful you decided to meet with me, Amber. I know how angry you were this morning," Morta said as she crossed the room and sank into the chair behind her desk.

"Really? You know how angry I was? I find that hard to believe, Morta, considering you asked me to be here right now."

Morta met her eyes. There was something there that Amber had never seen before, but she wasn't sure how to define it. It wasn't exactly sorrow or frustration. It wasn't even remorse. But, it did give her pause.

"Why am I here, Morta?" she asked.

"After this morning, I wanted to clear the karma."

"The karma?"

"You and I have been off kilter since this whole fiasco with Spade began, and I wanted to ensure that we were on the same page," she responded. She unlocked a tablet and shoved it across the desk towards Amber. "As you can see, I've taken the liberty of drawing up an agreement that I think you will find to be quite generous."

Amber flipped through the pages in the document Morta had pulled up for her review.

"Please tell me this is a joke," she whispered.

"It's not."

Amber glared at her over the top of the tablet. "You're just like everyone else. Just like my uncle!"

Morta shook her head, her expression impassive. "No, dear, I am nothing like your uncle. If there is anything I learned from this morning's attack, it is that even I am not immortal. No matter how much I want to believe that I am." She sighed as she motioned for Amber to sit. "From the moment I plucked you off the streets when you first arrived on Thoth, we have had something more than the typical employer-employee relationship, have we not?"

"Yes, but—"

"—But nothing. You might not believe me, Amber. And, that's fine. You don't have to. I have come to view you as more as a daughter than anything else. I want the Underworld, and all its assets, to be yours if anything happens to me."

"You're just trying to keep me here."

"Check the date, Amber. I signed this document months ago. Before we began negotiations with Spade. I've told you before that I was grooming you to take over after me. I just didn't expect to make it official so soon."

Amber scrolled to the end of the document and looked at the verified timestamp. She was telling the truth. She'd signed the will over six months ago.

"Why me?" she asked. Her fingers went numb as coldness spread through her body. Her mind flipped through all the times she and Morta had been alone over the past few months. It was difficult for her to believe that this was real. That it wasn't a ploy to trap her.

"I told you. You've become like a daughter to me. You should know that I rarely show affection to anyone. As to why you…it's difficult to say. But, it's probably because I see a little of myself in you."

Amber was at a loss for words. She felt like she was missing something, but didn't know what. She didn't even have the words to begin that conversation. To ask the right questions.

"I need time to think. To process. I'm sorry," she managed to get out.

"I understand."

Amber set the tablet on the table and turned to leave. When her back was to Morta she closed her eyes and sucked in a deep breath. The girl's unseeing eyes filled her vision, and she knew she couldn't leave without finding out what Morta knew about the experiments.

"You promised me you would tell me about the death house. So, tell me."

"You really do think I'm a monster, don't you?" Morta asked.

Amber couldn't tell if it was rhetorical or not. "I need to know," was all she said.

"If you honestly think that I would ever condone such behaviors, you don't know me at all," Morta replied bitingly. "The reason I was so focused on acquiring Spade was to stop the experiments, Amber. I told you before that there are things happening beyond my control. The war for our rights—for our lives—is still waging, and I will never give up until NAs have the same rights as everyone else."

Amber spun around, "Then why be so cryptic with me? Why not just say all of this when I asked you before?"

Morta shrugged. "There's so much you don't know yet about life." She held up her hands, placatingly. "I know, you've had a rough go of it, Amber. You've been through a lot, and I am truly sorry for the tragedies you've experienced. But, what you saw in that house is just a fraction of what has been happening to NAs since the official war ended. We are still seen as less than human."

Grinding her teeth, Amber considered her words. She didn't know how much she trusted Morta, but there was something about the vigor in her voice that gave her pause.

"I want to believe you, Morta—"

"—then do."

Amber shook her head. "How can I? It's only after I threaten to leave that you tell me all of this. That you offer me the keys to your kingdom." She closed her eyes again. "I'm still not sure I want to stay here. I can't make any promises."

"I don't need promises. I need an heir. And that's you."

"You're not listening to me! I'm saying I'm not sure that I can be that for you. Not anymore. All the death. All the threats on my life. The bodies—" she trailed off, still unsure how to express her feelings.

"You promised me this morning that you would remain until the contract with Spade was completely finalized. Give it the next few days to think about, Amber. I know you will come to the right decision."

Amber released a shuddering breath. Her shoulders sagged. She opened her mouth to supply a retort, but stopped short when she realized she didn't know what she wanted to say. She strode from the room without another word. She didn't know what the right decision was. Of if there was one at all.

Chapter Seventeen

Amber's bracelet pinged the moment she left Morta's office. Inwardly, she groaned, but accepted the text message anyway.

"I need to see you. It's urgent."

She stopped dead in her tracks. It was from another unknown number. Certain that it was the same caller from before, she quickly typed a response.

"No can do, motherfucker. You really think that I'd trust you again after you tried to have me killed? Better luck next time."

She hit send without rereading the message. She didn't have time to waste on someone who just wanted to kill her. She didn't know who J was, but she wasn't going to give him the chance to fool her a second time.

"What do you mean someone tried to kill you?"

She stared at the holographic message for a moment. Her immediate response was to delete and block the number. Not that she knew what number it was since it came through as unknown.

Still, she wanted the chance to take back control over the situation.

"Look, I don't know who in the void you think you are, but I'm not interested, okay? Stop messaging me."

Her fingers flew over the keyboard as she typed. Whoever this person was, he—or she—could rot for all Amber cared. She was too exhausted to deal with any of it.

Her bracelet pinged again and she pulled it open, her frustration flaring.

"I promise I don't bite."

She rolled her eyes at the response before promptly deleting it. If whoever was messaging her wanted to meet her, they would have to seek her out in person.

She wandered outside. Clicking on her music, she began jogging down the street. She didn't look at anyone as she passed. All she could think about was the dead girl's facial expression, the attacks on her life, the mutilated bodies on the casino floor, and Morta's offer.

She couldn't believe that Morta was willing to give her everything. It was so out of character for her that it left an unsettled feeling in the pit of Amber's stomach. She didn't understand why Morta was attempting to do this now. She just kept coming back to her trying to exert control.

Her neck tingled as the hair all over her body began to rise. She turned around just in time to see a hooded figure wrap their hands around her neck. A short, soft squeak escaped her lips before her scream was cut off.

She kicked, trying to break free. Nothing worked. She licked and then bit her assailant's hand. Still they didn't break their hold on her neck. If this was going to be the way she died, she didn't want to go down without a fight.

Throwing her head back, she managed to take them by surprise. Her head cracked against their nose with a satisfying crunch. She smirked as she slammed her elbow into the person's gut, repeatedly. They grunted, but didn't loosen their hold.

She scratched at the person's hand, silently pleading the civilians milling about the street to notice her plight and provide aid.

None of them did.

Everything went dark as a bag was pulled down over her head. Her hands were bound behind her back by what felt like a magnetized cuff. A gag was tied around her mouth. Its cloth bit into the corners of her lips, making them feel numb. She closed her eyes, anticipating what was to come.

Her death.

For a moment, she considered what it would be like: to give up. To not care about the world or its inhabitants.

To just be.

She decided that it wasn't worth it. Sure, she could do all those things, but she didn't want to. She wanted to keep fighting. It's what she always had done.

Her stabilizers ran rivers of heat up her arms as she concentrated on escaping. It was the vaguest sense of a plan, but she knew that her abilities would kick into gear once she initiated them.

Someone picked her up and threw her over his shoulder. Blood rushed to her head. There was a moment of disorientation and dizziness before she regained her focus again.

They carried her for several moments before she heard the distinctive pop of a door being opened. They threw her into what she could only assume was the backseat of a car before the low rumble of the engines igniting began and she felt the vehicle lift from the ground.

Although her hands were bound, they hadn't done the same to her feet. She twisted in the seat, using her legs to feel her way around. She was alone. She began kicking at the front seats.

"Stop that!" a male voice shouted.

She kicked again.

"I don't want to have to stun you, Fortuna," a feminine voice said.

Amber stilled. Well, that answered that question. There was more than one of them. With her stabilizers like fire in her veins, she kicked in the direction of the woman's voice.

"What the—"

She heard the woman say, presumably as she attempted to fire her pulser pistol, before Amber felt her foot connect with something softer. The woman grunted as hot liquid fell on Amber's leg.

She kicked again, harder this time and heard the distinctive sound of something crunching. She hoped it was the woman's nose and not something else.

She began focusing her kicks towards where she thought the man was. She hit the front seat several times, but couldn't seem to get past it.

"He told us you'd be a problem," the man said. "So, we came prepared."

"I think she broke my nose," the girl whined.

"I'll heal you when we get to the drop-off," the man responded.

Amber drooled onto the hood, unable to fully close her mouth. The corners of her lips ached from being pulled open by the gag. Frustrated, she rammed her head forward in an attempt to headbutt the girl, but she slammed into something hard and unbending.

The girl chuckled softly. "You're a real fighter, aren't ya?" she asked. "Well, we haven't lost a bounty yet, and I doubt you'll be the first. Not even your luck will be able to get you out of this one."

Amber released a guttural growl. It was the only noise she could make with the gag still firmly in her mouth.

"Leave her be, Calliope," the man chided.

"Why? She won't be our problem once we make the drop." There was so much venom in the girl's words that Amber was taken aback.

"Because the boss didn't want her damaged, remember? He explicitly stated that he wanted her given to him unscathed."

"You take all the fun out of hunting bounties," she groaned.

Amber leaned forward until her forehead brushed the hard barrier. It was cold to the touch and the smell reminded her of days spent in the garage with her dad, working on vintage cars and airplanes. She breathed in deeply, letting herself wander into the lane of memory.

"Five minutes out," the man said.

Amber jolted. She wasn't sure she wanted to know who had placed a bounty on her head. The only people she could think of were the LaRues. But then, why would they order the bounty hunters not to harm her? It didn't make sense to her.

The car began to descend. Amber sucked in a breath as she felt the familiar rise of her stomach and the giddy feeling that followed. She hated flying.

The vehicle jostled as it landed.

"There he is," the man said. "Wait here. I'll take care of the girl."

"Don't try anything," the woman said. "My pistol jammed once. It won't again."

If Amber could have smirked, she would have. As if the reason the pistol had jammed in the first place was because of a true mechanical malfunction and not because of Amber's luck.

"Just to be on the safe side," she murmured.

There was a harsh thump on the top of Amber's head. She swayed for a moment before toppling over.

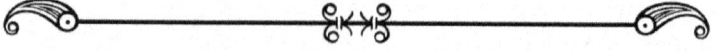

Amber jerked awake. She touched the top of her head gingerly. It was tender to the touch and she groaned softly. Memories of her kidnapping flooded back into her consciousness. Sitting up, she immediately began to sway as wooziness overtook her. She massaged her forehead, hoping to relieve some of the tension. It didn't help. And she was running out of time. She rolled off of the couch. The floor was like ice beneath her bare feet and she shivered.

Bookcases laden with texts covered the walls. Giant tapestries hung where bookcases wouldn't fit. A synthetic fire raged in the hearth. Its flames danced and writhed in a near-perfect pattern as Amber stared into it. She took a step forward. Pain exploded in her head and she winced.

"I'm so happy you're awake," a voice said from behind her.

Amber spun around, her heart racing. Her ability hadn't warned her someone was approaching. So, either she'd lost her abilities again, or he wasn't a threat. Her eyes widened when she saw J standing by a doorway, a mug of steaming liquid in his hand.

"I'm sorry I wasn't here when you woke up, but I needed some tea." He nodded towards the mug. "Would you like some? I'd be happy to make some for you." He smiled at her.

"What. In. The. Actual. Stars," she hissed, taking a step back. "Where are we? What am I doing here?"

He lifted a hand. "I'm sorry I had to bring you here this way, but when you declined my offer to meet, I knew I needed to get you here somehow."

She gaped at him, cursing herself for leaving her pulser pistol in her rooms back at Morta's home. "What do you want?"

He sighed. "Fortuna, I thought you trusted me."

"Yeah, I did. Until you tried to kill me!"

"Do you honestly think that was me?" he asked, taking a step towards her. "If I wanted to kill you, don't you think I would have done so while you were knocked unconscious?" he frowned, "I'm sorry about that, by the way. I explicitly told them not to cause any harm to you."

"You can't honestly think that I would believe you after you sent me to that café."

"What café?" he asked, his brown eyes brimming with concern. "I swear, I didn't message you before today."

She crossed her arms over her chest and took another step back. "I'm sorry, but I find that very difficult to believe."

"I regret it had to be this way," he continued. "But I couldn't stand the thought of you being in harm's way."

A tremble of fear ran through her. There was something about the way he said that last statement that made her feel like he knew something he wasn't telling her.

"What do you mean?" she asked.

"I thought it would have been obvious," he said with a smirk. "The conflict between Morta and the LaRues has come to a head. I know they tried to kill her this morning. I also know that they've figured out a way to block NA abilities."

Amber's heart leapt to her throat. She wondered if he knew she'd been without her abilities for a time only the day before. Nervously, she clenched her hands and waited for him to explain further. When he didn't, she asked, "How do they block other people's abilities?"

He shrugged. "Rumor has it that it's some sort of ingestible pill. They found an NA who could block other's abilities. They killed him for his DNA."

His tone was bitter and, Amber remembered the way he'd reacted at the house. He'd seemed callous to her then, but listening to the rage coating his words now, she wondered if his reaction at the house had simply been a defense mechanism.

She retraced her steps from the time she received the message to the time she followed the boy into the tunnels beneath Spade. She'd bumped into a few people on the way to the coffee shop. She'd ordered a hot chocolate. And then the boy showed up. A thought clicked into place.

"You said the drug was ingestible. Do you know how long it takes to go into effect? Or how long it lasts?"

"No. Why? Are you thinking about drugging someone in particular?" he waggled his eyebrows at her.

She scowled. He'd kidnapped her. Told her that Morta's life was still in danger. Oh, and he'd just revealed that they had the ability to block NA capabilities. She wasn't in the mood for him to flirt with her.

"Tell me everything you know," she demanded.

"Didn't even get a smile out of you," he grimaced. "Fine. What do you want to know?"

"Let's start with what you know about the attack the LaRues are planning."

"It's happening today. In less than an hour if I had to be accurate."

"What!"

"Calm down, Fortuna," he said, placing a firm hand on her arm. "There's nothing you can do."

"What do you mean?" she hissed.

"I've taken you someplace safe. Someplace far enough out of town they'll stop looking for you before they find you."

"Why? Why would you do this?"

"I thought it would be obvious," he said with a lopsided smile.

She shook her head.

"I care about you, Fortuna."

"You care about me!" she repeated, cutting him off. "Of all the asinine things I've heard recently, that has got to the be worst. Stars, J! I don't even know your real name. And you don't know mine."

"I know enough about you to know that this is real. It takes a lot for me to like someone, much less trust them. But with you…" He trailed off.

She shook her head. "It's never going to happen. Do you hear me? You took away my choice." She ran her hands through her hair as the realization struck her. There was an attack planned on the Underworld, and she wasn't there to stop it. She wouldn't be there to save them.

"You have to take me back. Now!" she commanded.

"I'm afraid I can't do that. Let me clarify, I won't do that."

She slapped him across the cheek. A bright red mark sprouted across his skin. He rubbed at his jaw for a moment. "Nice hit," he said, seemingly unphased by her outburst.

"Please, J, you have to let me go back. I need to be with her. I can protect her."

"You're not strong enough to take on the whole LaRue family. Trust me when I say that the safest place for you is right here. I don't want them getting their hands on your ability."

She began pacing across the room. A part of her knew he was right. But that didn't mean she had to admit it to him.

"J," she whispered, turning towards him.

"Fortuna," he responded, a smile touching his lips.

She shrugged it off. It didn't matter if he felt like there was this deep connection between them.

"I might be at odds with Morta right now. If fact, I may very well despise her. But, that doesn't change the fact that I chose her as my family. She's my person, J. I can't just let her die with no warning."

He stared at her for several moments. "Fortuna, let me be clear with you. I can't let you leave."

"Why not?" she demanded.

"I can't imagine Morta would want you to put yourself in harm's way. Not if she knew what was coming."

"So, warn her!" Amber shouted. "Call her right now and tell her to prepare. Please, J. I'm begging you."

He shrugged. "I know you won't believe me when I tell you that I wish I could give you everything you ask for. But I can't. It doesn't work like that. It is unrealistic."

She rolled her eyes at him. "Then make it realistic."

"The best I can offer you is to watch what happens through an aerial drone."

Her mouth dropped open slightly at his suggestion. "I don't want to watch her get injured or killed, J! I want to save her!"

"Take it or leave it, the choice is yours." He turned from her then. The muscles in his back rippled as he strode away from her.

She caught his wrist in her hand and tugged him towards her. "Who are you really?" she asked.

"A friend."

Her grasp on him tightened. "Tell me the truth. Who. Are. You?"

The back of her neck tingled. She reacted a fraction too late as a gust of wind buffeted her. She stumbled, but he caught her before she fell. The wind died down to nothing more than a low whistle around the corner.

"If I wanted to harm you, Fortuna, I could. But that's not what I want. What I most desire is for you to trust me. To let me be the weirdo that sooths your pains, makes you laugh, and walks hand-in-hand with you through life's adventures."

"What the stars, J!" Intellectually, she understood what he was saying, and there had been an attraction between them, but this was ludicrous. She trailed her hands over his body until they were square on his chest. He leaned down. His eyes smoldered and he licked his lips. She rolled her eyes at him just as she shoved him, hard, in the chest. He stumbled backwards with a grunt.

"You don't even know my real name, and you're making it sound like you're in love with me. Fuck that. I don't have the time or patience."

He placed his hands on her shoulders. "I am trying my best to protect you."

"I don't need your protection," she sniffed, lifting her chin higher. "What I need is to help the people I love. If you're not going to help me do that, then you're an enemy."

He glowered at her for a moment. He opened his mouth to speak just as a voice interrupted them from seemingly thin air.

"Sir, sorry for the intrusion, but shots were fired on the corner of Xilon and Calcipher."

Amber's heart dropped to the pit of her stomach. Those were the cross streets outside of the entrance to the Underworld. She met J's gaze, pleading for him to let her go. For a moment, she thought he would acquiesce. There was tenderness and concern in his eyes. And something else she couldn't quite place.

His face darkened as the voice piped in again, "Confirmed casualties."

Chapter Eighteen

Amber clenched her fists tightly as she tried to control her breathing. People were dying. Again. And she wasn't there to help.

"You have to let me go. Now!" she screamed.

J shook his head. There was a finality to the movement that made her skin crawl. Who was he to tell her what she could and couldn't do?

"The best I can do is fly a drone over the street fight. You'll be able to watch what happens."

"That's not good enough!" She scanned the room, anxious for any way out. The only exit she found was the door directly behind where J was standing. To get to it, she would need to get past him.

Her stabilizers engaged, sending a wave of heat up her arms as she contemplated racing past him. She didn't know how far out of the 'V' she was, but she was determined to make it back. Even if she was too late—

She stopped herself from considering what would happen. She couldn't think about that now. Maybe never, if she was successful.

She lunged forward just as a gust of wind propelled her backwards.

"I can do this all day," J said, his hands trembling slightly.

She glared at him. "If you do this and Morta dies, I will never forgive you. Do you understand me? Never."

He closed his eyes and heaved in a massive sigh. The vein his neck pulsed, and Amber could tell that he was struggling to say whatever it was that he really wanted to. Finally, he met her gaze with eyes wide open.

"I'm sorry, Fortuna. This is one fight that you cannot—will not—win."

The door began to glaze over with ice. Layer upon layer was added until it was like looking through a frosted pane of glass. Amber seethed as she plopped into a chair.

"Send the drone," she commanded, dejectedly.

"Already on its way."

She rolled her eyes at him. His response was just one more reason to dislike him. He was so cocky in his ability to stop her from leaving his home that'd he'd preemptively sent the drone.

"Sir," the voice said, "Justine LaRue is requesting a vid conference."

Amber's eyebrows rose. If he wasn't in league with the LaRues, why would their leader want to conference chat with him. She ground her teeth to stop herself from saying anything.

"Tell her I'm busy," he replied. He met her gaze from across the room. "And Merlin, please update my status as 'do not contact,' for the foreseeable future."

"Yes, sir," the voice replied.

"Merlin?" Amber asked, intrigued.

"My AI," J replied absent-mindedly as he created a holographic keyboard in front of him and began typing away. His brow furrowed as he entered code into the system.

"What are you doing?" she asked, her curiosity getting the better of her.

"I am pulling all the vid files from nearby security cameras so that you can have a 360 degrees vantage point."

"Hey, you know what would be even better than that?" she paused, waiting to see if he would take the bait. When he didn't, she mumbled, "Letting me leave."

"Sorry, can't," he replied without looking up from the screen.

She tapped her fingers on the chair's arm, unsure of what to say. Holographic images materialized all around the room as J pulled the security footages' livestream. A high-definition image spread across the middle of the room. She could tell by the way it moved that it was the live-feed from the drone.

Leaning forward, she squinted at the tiny dots scurrying across the bottom of the screen. Blasts of brilliant light exploded across the display as plasma rifles were fired. Electric blue streaks flew through the air where high-velocity darts struck their targets.

She gasped. She hadn't anticipated so many people to be involved in the battle.

"Can you show me a closer up image?" she whispered. Her chest ached as she searched the battlefield for any sign of Morta.

"Give me a sec," he responded. She could already hear the flurry of his fingers on the keyboard.

One of the screens morphed into a magnified view. A guard wearing Morta's insignia was locked in hand-to-hand combat with one of Spade's thugs. They appeared to be evenly matched as they grappled with each other. Amber found herself leaning in closer. She held her breath as the Spade representative landed a blow to his opponent's temple. The man's eyes turned glassy as he fell to the ground.

"How many casualties?" Amber breathed. From what she could tell, there were more of the Underworld's people laying on

163

the ground than those of Spade's. If she had to guess, Guinevere, or another luck-driver, was there, manipulating the battle to favor Spade. She bit her bottom lip in an attempt to stop herself from saying as much to J.

"Merlin," J said, "How many dead so far?"

"Sixty, as of 30 seconds ago," the AI responded.

"So many," she whispered, leaning back into the chair. Her breathing became shallow and her stomach felt as if she were going to hurl at any moment. She needed to be there, and if J couldn't understand that, then he was not her friend.

"J, if you love me at all, you will let me go. I need to help."

"It's too late," he said, pointing at one of the screens. "You'll never get there in time."

Amber jerked her head towards the vid display in question. Morta, wearing a tight, leather outfit swept down the street. Wisps of opal luminescence swirled from Spade's soldiers as she strode past them. Amber had never seen her absorb another human's energy like that before. Normally, she needed physical contact. But now, she sucked their life-force from them as if they were nothing more than gusts of wind.

Dozens of soldiers fell in her wake.

A brave, or stupid, Spade soldier rushed towards Morta. The barrel of her pulser pistol glowed red. Amber screamed as a series of darts erupted from the muzzle, streaking light behind them as they raced through the air.

Three of them struck Morta in the back. She stumbled forward as she released a cry of pain. Shrapnel left ragged holes across the front of her shirt. Crimson blood was already pooling at her feet as she slowly sank to her knees.

"No!" Amber screamed. She reached towards the holographic image. Although, cognitively, she knew she couldn't touch Morta, the impulse to protect her was overwhelming.

She stopped breathing as Morta lifted her chin to look at a figure approaching from farther down the street. Amber recognized the man as Laurie LaRue. His face was hard and impassive as he stared down at Morta.

His lips moved, but the audio was too low for the drone's microphone to pick up. Her flesh crawled as he lifted a pulser pistol and rested the barrel against Morta's forehead.

In that moment, Amber could only think about saving her. Her stabilizers blazed to life as she concentrated on the single, permeating thought of rescuing Morta from this situation. She knew she was too far away. She knew her abilities had never extended that far before. But she couldn't stop herself.

As if in slow motion, she watched as Laurie depressed the trigger. Her arms burned with fire. Still, she continued to focus on the single thought of saving Morta. Pain exploded in her mind as she envisioned something, anything rescuing her from the dart that would inevitably strike her.

A brilliant explosion filled the screen as it zoomed in on the barrel of the pistol. Smoke made it impossible to see what had happened. Amber released a breath as she collapsed to the ground. Her head banged against a coffee table on her way down.

She glanced up at the screen in time to see Laurie LaRue's mangled hand dripping blood, and Morta wrapping her arms around his neck. His essence seeped from him and was absorbed into her. The wounds on her back slowly stopped leaking blood as more and more of his soul was transferred to her.

A smirk crested Amber's lips as she let her exhaustion overpower her. She didn't understand how she'd done it, but she knew she had. She'd saved Morta.

Amber awoke to the sound of explosions. Groggily, her eyes fluttered open, and she stared up at the ceiling. Light streaked across holographic screens, causing a wave of nausea to wash over her. She coughed as she sat up.

Her muscles felt as if she had been lifting too-heavy weights for days. She lifted her arm to massage her shoulder muscles but was too weak to keep it up for more than a few seconds before needing to let it drop again.

"What?" she mumbled, her words catching in the back of her throat.

J crouched before her. He frowned as he placed a cool hand on her forehead.

"What happened?" she attempted again. This time the words formed properly.

"Shh," he murmured as he scooped her into his arms and cradled her to his chest. "Don't waste your energy."

He walked with her towards the door. The ice melted as if it were bearing the brute force of the sun.

"Wait!" she said, panic swelling within her. She needed to know what happened. The sound of more explosions drew her attention back to the vid displays. The flurry of movement made her stomach squirm, but she forced herself to look on.

She saw Morta. Engaged in a battle with Guinevere and Frost. Jasper had his back pressed against her, protecting her from behind. Bella was there, too. Her face was scrunched together as she concentrated on using her fire.

"Please," she begged when J didn't stop heading towards the door. "I have to see."

He stared at her for a long moment before finally nodding and turning around so that they could both watch the events unfolding on the screen.

Frost's blue cybernetic eye blazed as gusts of winter wind buffeted Bella, Jasper, and Morta. Ice formed on the tips of Morta's fingers as she stretched out her arms towards him, clearly attempting to steal his soul. Flickers of his life energy writhed towards her, slowly merging with her hand.

From this angle, Amber saw a small, lithe figure dart from the shadows. They flung themselves across the short distance to Morta and jabbed a syringe into the other woman's neck.

The light emanating from Frost immediately snuffed out. Amber watched, horrified as Guinevere aimed her plasma rifle at Morta and fired.

Chapter Nineteen

Amber stared at the screen. Unseeing. Unfeeling.

Limp.

She couldn't believe the charred, smoking body on the ground was Morta.

Numbly she clung to J.

He kissed her brow. Rubbed circles across her shoulders and back. Whispered that everything was going to be okay.

She didn't believe him.

Nothing was okay.

Nothing would ever be okay again.

She just continued to stare.

Bella's fire surrounded Frost. His blue eye dimmed as her flames engulfed him.

A shadow erupted from Jasper's back and flowed across the street until it wrapped itself around Guinevere. Her face contorted into pure pain as the shadow strangled her. Her eyes bulged as she grasped at her throat, unable to get a hold on the shadow.

Soldiers rushed forward, forming a circle around Morta. A ballistic shield established a perimeter.

Amber knew it was too little, too late.

The charred body.

Her shoulders wracked as she attempted to hold back the scream. Tears flowed freely from her eyes.

This couldn't be it.

But she knew it was.

A guttural wail erupted from her. Over and over. She cried. Weakly, she pounded her fists against J's chest.

She'd unlocked a new dimension to her power. She'd manipulated the firing mechanism on the puler pistol. She'd saved Morta from Laurie.

It hadn't been enough.

She hadn't been strong to save her.

J held a cloth to her nose. She breathed in deeply before she could stop herself. There was a putrid scent followed by a hazy, warm feeling as she slipped into unconsciousness.

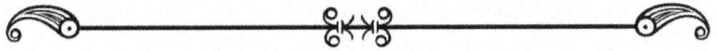

She woke to the clicking of fingers on keys. For a moment, she didn't know where she was. She sat up too quickly, the blood rushing from her head and leaving her dizzy. She peered around the dimly lit room.

Curtains billowed slightly from a phantom breeze. She lay on an old-fashioned four-poster bed with sheer curtains encircling her. Through the haze, she could see J hunched over a desk, wildly tapping away. Paintings hung on the walls.

She breathed in and out. Sat in her own fatigue and numbness.

The image of the charred body shoved itself to the forefront of her mind.

Morta was gone.

Clenching her fists, Amber pulled back the curtain surrounding the bed and lunged towards J. Her legs were still weak from whatever he'd used to drug her, and she stumbled. Her chin slammed into the back of his chair as she fell forward. She tasted hot copper as she bit her tongue.

"The effects will wear off in a few more hours," J said, without breaking his concentration from the screen.

Gingerly, she prodded at her already swelling mouth. She wasn't used to physical injuries since her ability protected her from harm most of the time.

"I'll take you home once you've regained your strength," he continued.

She punched him on the side. He flinched slightly, but didn't respond.

"Look at me!" she demanded.

He finished typing a last string of code before stretching his arms out before him. His joints popped faintly as he pulled his fingers outward and held the position for several seconds. Then, he peered down at her, an expression of mild curiosity on his face.

"Yes, dear," he said.

It took all her willpower not to smack him in his smart mouth. He was the reason Morta was dead. If she had been there, if she hadn't extended herself in saving her the first time, maybe—most definitely—Morta would still be alive.

"I want to go home now," she said.

He brushed his fingertips over her forehead. The corners of his mouth drooped. "You're not quite well enough—"

"You are not my owner, J. You don't get to tell me when I can and cannot do things. Take me back to the Underworld or—"

"Or what? You'll report me to the authorities?" he smirked at her. "You and I both know that you would rather eat durfian dung than do that."

She breathed out heavily through her nose and pierced him with a wild, angry stare. She motioned between them, "We are not friends, J. You kidnapped me! Do you realize what you've done? Morta is dead because of you!"

All the smugness left his expression at her words. "You want to be angry, fine, be angry. But I will not allow you to blame her death on me. She was stupid enough to start a war against the powers that be, and it cost her everything."

Amber slapped him. Her hand stung and her arm felt as if she had been carrying a plasma rifle for hours. A thin, pink line blossomed on his cheek where she'd struck him.

"Was that really necessary?" he asked, rubbing his jaw.

"I don't want to be here anymore. Either take me home now, or I promise you, I will report you to the police."

He stared at her. At first a look of wry bemusement covered his face, but the longer he held her gaze, the more it morphed into an expression of contemplation.

"Fine," he finally said. "I'll arrange for Merlin to provide transport back to the Underworld."

"Your AI can drive?" she asked.

He shrugged. "I designed a body for him and taught him to do all sorts of things. I built him myself."

"Oh."

They sat in silence for several moments. Amber remained on the floor. She still felt woozy and was afraid that if she moved, she would collapse entirely. Sometimes it is better to let things ride than force them into submission.

"Can you, at the very least, tell me who you really are?" she asked. She wasn't sure why she wanted to know.

"How do I know you won't try to kill me—or worse—ruin me if I tell you?" he asked.

She shrugged. "I think we're past the point where you should be worrying about that. You kidnapped me. Stopped me from saving Morta. Forced me to sit back and watch as everything I loved was destroyed. Trust when I say that if I wanted to kill you, it wouldn't be because I discovered your real identity."

He laughed. He laughed so hard, in fact, that his whole body shook.

Amber scowled at him. "Really? That's how you respond?"

He shrugged. "You're cute when you're angry."

Her glare deepened. "You do realize that you're hitting on me right after I tell you that you've ruined my life."

"I didn't ruin your life, Fortuna. I kept you out of harm's way."

She sighed. "Agree to disagree." She scooted backwards and out of his reach. "Your name," she prodded.

"James."

"James what?"

"Li."

Her skin tingled at the name. She'd heard it before, but she wasn't sure where. "Why do I know that name?" she asked. She didn't think she'd ever heard it mentioned before, but her ability flared as if she was supposed to know something about him.

"Oh, you know, infamous gambler and charlatan. The great Don Juan. King of Taurus."

She blinked at him. "King of Taurus," she paused, "The King...You're the King?"

"And I thought you would have figured it out faster than that."

She stuttered over her words. She couldn't believe that this arrogant, cocky, kidnapper could be the leader of the Taurus Syndicate. He was a mystery to everyone. Few knew what he looked like. Fewer still knew his real name.

"I don't understand," she began.

"Mort and I go way back," he said. "She was my first friend when I landed on Thoth, similar to you. Though, I must say, I was significantly younger than you when I was brought here. She helped me distinguish myself." He turned away from her, his voice cracking slightly as he continued. "She asked me to help her in the fight against the LaRues and the ones backing them. I declined."

"Then why—"

He held up a finger, stilling her lips as he continued, "Then I saw you. I don't know how to explain it, but I knew then that you and I were meant to do great things together."

She rolled her eyes at him. "You don't even know me," she whispered. "How can you believe that we're supposed to fulfill some great destiny if you don't even know who I am?"

"Call it intuition," he shrugged. "The point is, Morta asked me to ensure your safety if I sensed something was about to happen."

Amber stilled. Her heart pounded in her chest and she took short, shallow breaths. She doubted Morta would have trusted one of her rivals to protect her. And, she certainly didn't believe the bit about James seeing her and knowing from first sight that they would 'achieve great things together.' If that was true, he was more delusional than she thought.

She rose to her feet. Swaying slightly as her legs absorbed her weight, she rested her hand on the couch.

"Even if I did believe you, and I'm not saying I do, why would I trust you now? Taurus was the largest gambling syndicate on Thoth. You own more upscale casinos than any of the others. Well, you did, anyway." She smirked at him. "Now that the Underworld has acquired Spade, I guess that makes Morta's syndicate the largest."

"And you the new queen," he replied, a smug smile stretched across his face. "Or did you forget that Morta named you her heir."

Amber's hands dropped to her sides at his words. "How did you know she offered—"

"She didn't just offer. She explicitly named you. I saw the paperwork myself."

She gaped at him. She didn't understand how that was possible. Morta had showed her the will only a few hours before the fighting began. There hadn't been time for her to show them to James.

"I can tell you're trying to figure this all out. All I can tell you is that I have sensed something would happen to Morta for a very long time now. I told her of my concerns, and she made me promise to protect you. Of course, she didn't know that I had already decided I would do the latter."

It was too much for her to think about now. Every time she closed her eyes, flashes of Morta's charred body mixed with the dead girl's eyes. Her father's wheezing, last breath. The smell of decay.

All she wanted to do was curl into a little ball and sink into sleep. Maybe when she woke, the nightmare would be over. One could hope.

"Please," she finally said, "just take me home."

His lips parted as if he were going to say something else, thought better of it, and then shut it again.

"I promise I'll have guards posted outside my room. I just—" she trailed off, unsure how to say what she was feeling. "I just need to be home."

He nodded. "I can understand that," he finally said. "As I said, I'll arrange for Merlin to drive you—"

"You won't take me?" she asked. Her hand twitched at the question. She didn't know where that had come from.

His eyes widened, and his cheeks flushed a light pink. "Are you sure that's what you want?"

"Yes," she whispered.

His expression vacillated between a deep hunger and confusion. Amber cocked an eyebrow at him, amused by the clearly warring emotions he was experiencing.

"Fine," he finally barked out.

He turned to face the screen again, his fingers already tapping on the keyboard. "But I'm going to check on the status of survivors. What happened today was a verifiable bloodbath."

His words left Amber's insides in knots. The last she'd seen Jasper and Bella were still alive. But, that didn't mean they still were. The fighting had continued after Morta's death. She didn't

174

know for how long, but she knew that she hadn't wanted any part of it.

"Merlin, pull medic reports for the LaRues and," he glanced back at her, "anyone else Fortuna requests information on."

"Of course, sir," the AI replied. "Miss Fortuna," it said, drawing her attention back to him, "are there specific people you want me to search the medical database for?"

"Er, yes," she said, hesitantly. She wanted to know if Jasper and Bella had survived. And Frost. He might have been a major pain in her ass for the duration of the negotiation, but she'd seen him outside of work, too. He was fun and intelligent. And, he had saved her life. Or course, that could have all been a ploy to get her to trust him, but still. It had worked.

She provided the AI with her short list of names and waited while Merlin went away to data mine. It only took him a few minutes to return to the screen.

"All humans listed survived."

"What!" she whirled toward James. "How is that possible? Do you still have the vid feed? I need to see what happened."

Her hands were clammy. She knew what she had seen. Frost died in a ball of flames, and Guinevere was strangled by Jasper's shadow. There was no possible way they'd survived.

James tapped a file on the holographic screen, and a series of videos populated the space before them. There were at least eight different angles. Amber's jaw dropped open as she saw Thoth's police force storm into the street seconds after the guards surrounded Morta's body. They tackled Jasper and Bella to the ground and tased them.

Amber's gaze was drawn to movement at the bottom of the frame, and she turned her attention to the guards surrounding Morta. They scattered as the police approached them. Amber's eyes widened as she realized that the body was no longer there.

"Where'd she go?" she asked, her voice tight and pitched.

James rewound the vid file by a few minutes and clicked play again. Amber trained her eyes on the spot she'd last seen Morta's body. The guards surrounded it. A flash of bright light from a plasma rifle distorted the frame for a second. But the guards were still there. She watched until they scattered when the police force arrived.

"I don't understand," Amber whispered as James clicked a button to slow down the pace of the vid file. They watched in slow motion again. And then a third time. Still, Amber couldn't find any sign for where Morta's body had gone. The only anomaly in the entire file was the burst of light from the rifle, but it didn't look like any of the guards had moved.

Fuming, she asked James if there was an angle that better showed what happened between Frost, Guinevere, Jasper, and Bella. He pulled up security footage from one of the Underworld's cameras.

She watched as Guinevere pulled the trigger on her plasma rifle. She didn't look away this time as Morta's body burst into flame and collapsed to the ground as a charred lump. Tears burned her eyes; she let them silently fall as she continued watching. Bella enclosed Frost in a curtain of flame. His cybernetic eye dimmed as he was completely engulfed.

She watched as Jasper's shadow tackled Guinevere and began choking her. It was difficult and yet oddly satisfying to watch the other luck-driver struggle to keep herself alive. The conflict of emotions left Amber feeling oddly guilty, although she didn't know why.

The police rushed in, tasing both Jasper and Bella. Bella's flames snuffed out, and Jasper's shadow dissolved into nothingness.

Although Frost had scorch marks all along his face and his clothes were singed and blackened, he appeared to have been able to shield himself with his powers enough to reduce the damage. Guinevere clutched at her throat. If Amber had to take a guess, she would bet that her windpipe had been bruised by the shadow's grip.

Her gaze followed Guinevere until she left the camera's frame.

She had murdered Morta.

Bile rose up the back of her throat. She didn't care what it took. She wanted revenge. The LaRues had taken away the one person since her parents died who had showed an ounce of care for her.

She would make them pay.

Chapter Twenty

Amber paced Morta's rooms. It had been two days since the massacre on Calcipher Ave. That's what people were calling it. Over one hundred were dead, distributed evenly between those loyal to Morta and those who served the LaRues.

Thoth's police force were struggling to track down the ones responsible for the killing. Witnesses claimed that the Underworld attacked first. Other say the LaRues charged in with pistols and rifles blazing. She'd asked James to supply the police with the vid files he'd captured that day, but he'd refused, stating that he'd already wiped them clean so as to protect the identities of the NAs.

She doubted the veracity of his claim.

He'd received a vid call from Justine LaRue during the battle. And, if she wasn't mistaken, had received multiple messages from the hag hours after the massacre ended as well. He could claim he'd kidnapped her to protect her. He could plead his case that Morta had entrusted him to watch over her.

But she didn't believe him. Or trust him.

For all she knew, he was just another pawn in Justine's plans.

She snatched up her baton and flipped it in her hand. She caught a glimpse of herself in Morta's mirror. Dark bags were under her red eyes from all the crying she'd done over the past two days. Her hair was limp and dull. Her scars prominent beneath the tattoos covering her forearms.

She dropped the baton into its holster and double-checked that her pulser pistol was secure in the holster at her hip. She lifted the lid to Morta's jewelry box and lifted the interior box out to reveal the secret compartment beneath. A sad smiled crept over her lips as she pulled out a pair of twin blades from the box.

Although small, they were razor-sharp. Emeralds and black diamonds encrusted their hilts. Amber depressed the miniscule button at the bottom of the hilt, and the blade on the first dagger began to burn with blue fire. She repeated the action on the second blade, which hummed with electricity.

Although the blades were meant to be more ornamental than functional, she'd given them to Morta only the year before as a birthday gift. They were hers now. Left to her in Morta's will.

She'd left everything to her.

The casinos. The money. The resorts on other planets.

Everything.

Amber wasn't sure how she was going to manage all her new responsibilities without Morta's advice.

She hadn't been able to sleep since she'd returned to the Underworld. Riddled with guilt that she'd ever believed Morta would have acquired Spade for the sole purpose of continuing the illegal research on the NAs, she tossed and turned all night.

A voice whispered in her mind that it was her fault.

If she hadn't argued with Morta. If she had given her a chance to explain herself, none of this would have happened. She would have been there to protect her.

Anger at James for stripping her of her choice to defend the Underworld and Morta was almost suffocating. She couldn't believe that she had been so stupid as to believe that he had been her friend.

She sighed heavily.

It didn't matter. She would extract her revenge on them all. Starting with Guinevere.

She slid the daggers into her boots and checked herself in the mirror one more time. She hoped Morta would be proud of the fighter she had become.

On a lark, she retrieved one of the death cards Morta made her deliver to her victims before leaving the bedroom. She stared down at the hollowed-out eyes. Fitting that it was the Ace of Spades.

The streets were silent as she made her way to Spade. She owned it now. The electronic paperwork had already been filed by the time the street fighting broke out. Both sets of signatures emblazoned on the contract. Closing would take place in another two days to give time for the remaining LaRue family members and their staff to move out of the facilities.

She'd asked James to hack into their system and discover which room Guinevere lived in. She didn't trust him not to alert the LaRue family that she was coming, but she didn't care if they knew or not.

Despite the lack of sleep, she felt confident. Strong.

Lucky.

She turned down an ally way and followed the crooked path until it dead-ended at a steel gate. She glanced to both sides before unholstering her pulser pistol and pressing the barrel against the gate's frame. Switching the dart to armor-piercing, she pulled the trigger.

A loud kaboom rang in her ears, and she coughed as dust and smoke filled her lungs. Her eyes watered, and she felt dizzy for a second as the concussive explosion hit her.

Closing her eyes, she focused on her breathing. Her heart rate decreased and her mind cleared. She'd come here for one reason: to kill Guinevere.

She ran through the mangled gate.

Her bracelet buzzed against her skin and a holographic diagram of Spade's blueprints popped up before her. She scanned the walkways until she found the tiny, purple dot indicating Guinevere's rooms.

She passed a few people as she raced through down the hallways. None of them stopped her, for which she was grateful. She didn't want to have to fight anyone else. Not even Frost. She just wanted to end the woman who'd taken Morta from her.

She rounded a corner and skidded to a halt. At the end of the hall was none other than Justine LaRue.

The matriarch was alone, her back to Amber. The faint blue glow of a tablet illuminated her face, but cast shadows all around her. Amber crept forward as silently as possible. Her heart thudded loudly in her ears.

She was less than one meter away from the other woman when Justine suddenly said, "I know why you're here, Amber Alcott."

Amber froze. How had Justine known her name? Had James betrayed her to the LaRues afterall?

She bit her lip to stop herself from responding.

"I don't care if you kill my luck-driver," Justine was saying. "Her usefulness has run out, anyway. The police will take her if you don't. She killed a wounded woman in cold blood, after all."

Slowly, Justine turned towards Amber, her blue eyes seemed to glow in the light from her tablet. She smiled at Amber.

"It's such a pity that you chose the wrong side," Justine said. "You could have done great things with us." She sighed as she closed the tablet and crossed her arms over her chest. "Morta always bragged about how you were one of the strongest little auggies she'd ever met." Her lips curled into a cold, cruel smile. "Too bad she never taught you how to properly control your abilities."

Amber took a step back, her hand instinctively landing on her pulser pistol. "What do you mean?"

"Isn't it obvious? I can sense the untapped wealth of power in you. Surely, you've sensed it yourself. How else do you explain how you're still alive?"

Amber remembered all the times people had manipulated her into doing their bidding. Used her abilities like she was a genie in a bottle, able to produce any desire they had. That's not how her ability worked. Or, at least, that's not how she wanted to use it.

She didn't consider herself a good person. Or a hero. She just wanted to survive and ensure the survival of those she cared about. Was that too much to ask? She didn't think so.

"I don't know what you think you know about me, Justine, and I don't really care. Your time on Thoth is over. Spade is mine. I'm the new queen in town." She started off so confidently, but the more the words came rushing out of her, the more she found herself thinking she sounded like a petulant, scared little girl. She snapped her mouth shut and waited for Justine to reply.

When she didn't, Amber continued, "I'm not here to kill you, Justine."

"As if you could."

Amber ignored the other woman's response. She'd come here for Guinevere. No one else.

"Leave Thoth and never come back. That's the price of your survival."

Justine shrugged. "I never wanted to come back to this void of a place anyway."

She stalked past Amber, her heels clicking on the metal floor. Amber watched her go, unsure how to respond. She hadn't been anticipating seeing the woman anyway.

"Oh, and by the way, I will leave you with two bits of information I'm sure you'll find most interesting," Justine said with a slight drawl. "Number one," she held up a single finger and smiled at Amber, "I drugged Guinevere's food tonight. Consider it a parting gift to you. She won't be able to use her cybernetic abilities to save herself. So, have at it."

Amber didn't know how to feel about that. She had anticipated in an even match between them. She didn't know if she wanted to win the fight just because she could manipulate the odds in her favor. Although it had never bothered her before, somehow, the fact that the other woman had been drugged to make this possible left her feeling icky about the whole situation.

"Two number," Justine continued, "your little friend, Teddy Marsh—AKA Frost—has been dealt with. You can thank him for your life."

Amber raised an eyebrow at the other woman. "What do you mean?"

"Didn't you wonder who drugged you that day in the café? Or why Frost knew where to find you?" she laughed viciously. "He disobeyed direct orders to save you."

"You were the one who ordered my death, then?" Amber hissed. This only confirmed what she had already suspected, but the fact that Justine was willingly offering her this tidbit of information made her uneasy. What game was the matriarch playing at?

Justine giggled. "Of course, it was me. Your little powers were becoming a nuisance that needed to be squashed. So, I arranged for one of my special pets to be waiting for you in the tunnels. With a little help from the café owner, it wasn't difficult to spike your drink with the debilitating serum."

"Why go through all that trouble just let me live now?" Amber asked. Her hackles rose as she glanced from side-to-side, anticipating an attack any moment.

"You're more useful to me alive than dead now that you're in-charge of both the Underworld and Spade."

"And why's that?"

"Because at some point, you will realize that your idealized version of Morta was wrong. She was a coward, Amber. A weak woman who fed on the fears of others. In time, you'll come to see that what we can offer you is more valuable than you can imagine right now."

"Uh huh. And you think, what? That I'm just going to accept your lies as truth right from the start? I know about your illegal tests on NAs, Justine. You and your family are monsters."

"Pft, such strong words for a child barely old enough to vote on galactic matters. You know nothing of this world, Amber."

Amber's lips snapped open as she prepared to deliver a sharp retort. But, she couldn't think of anything witty enough to say in response, so she simply turned away from Justine and whispered, "I will never be a part of whatever plan it is you have to replicate NA abilities in the ungifted," she said.

It was Justine's time to freeze. Her breathing became quick and shallow as she stared down the hallway at Amber, who took a step away from the other woman. She didn't know what the matriarch would do, but she doubted it would be pain free.

Justine shuddered, her cheeks flaring a brilliant red before she quickly crossed the divide between them and gripped Amber's chin between her fingers. The nails bit into her flesh, leaving her feeling powerless to defend herself. Her nostrils flared as she stared Amber straight in the eyes.

"One day, when you're begging me to let you have an audience with my employers, you'll think back on this day with regret, Amber. You are nothing in this world. A weakling who doesn't even know how voided she is." She released her hold on Amber and stepped away.

Amber didn't say anything as she watched the matriarch wander down the hall and slip around the corner. She didn't understand why she hadn't taken her shot. She could have killed her. Right there. It would have been over. But, something had stopped her.

Something to ponder later, she decided.

She checked the blueprints one last time to ensure herself that she was outside the correct room.

"I will avenge you, Morta," she whispered as she kicked in the door to Guinevere's room.

Guinevere turned towards Amber, a scowl on her face.

184

"What are you doing here?" she asked, her voice high-pitched and twangy.

Amber aimed her pulser pistol at her. Her arm shook as she set the dart selector on shrapnel blast instead of stun.

Guinevere laughed. "Do you honestly think you can beat me, Fortuna? Haven't I shown you that I am stronger than you already?" She strode across the room until her forehead was pressed against the barrel of Amber's pistol. "I'm not afraid of you. You couldn't even save your pathetic master. What makes you think that you can outmaneuver me now?"

Amber's finger twitched. She wanted to pull the trigger. To be done with it. She wanted the person who had taken Morta's life to suffer. To rid the universe of her. Yet, as she stared into the other woman's eyes, she couldn't bring herself to pull the trigger.

Guinevere wrapped her hands around Amber's, holding the pistol in place. "Go on," she hissed, "Do it."

Her finger on the trigger tightened. She could see it now. The shrapnel tearing through Guinevere's skull. Her brain matter splattered across the floor. The satisfaction she'd feel knowing that she'd extracted revenge for Morta.

This was what Morta had always wanted her to be. Strong. Unyielding. Willing to do whatever it takes for self-preservation.

To maintain her legacy.

Her name.

Morta.

Amber pulled the trigger.

Chapter Twenty-One

Amber's stabilizers burned beneath her skin as her pistol made a stranger chirping sound. She looked into Guinevere's eyes to see a look of triumph there.

Justine had lied to her after all.

Guinevere hadn't been drugged.

She still had her powers.

With a growl, she threw the pistol to the side, where the dart launched from the barrel and exploded into dozens of metal shards that lodged themselves into Guinevere's bed. Amber lunged for the other woman. Her stabilizers hummed as she pulled one of her daggers from her boot and swiped at Guinevere's side. The blade sliced a thin line across her abdomen, leaving a crimson trail.

"To think that you actually thought you were the luckiest woman alive. Who calls themselves 'Fortuna,' anyway?"

Guinevere mocked. "You were so smug, so full of yourself that you didn't even stop to consider how weak you actually are."

She threw a punch at Amber's temple, which Amber was able to dodge by scant centimeters.

"Void!" Guinevere exclaimed.

Amber engaged the button on the bottom of the dagger, and blue flame swirled around the blade. She flipped the blade in her hand and feigned a strike to the left. At the last moment, Amber changed course and drove the dagger into Guinevere's side, right above her hip bone.

The other woman screamed as Amber wrenched the blade free, and blood flowed freely from the wound.

"You were saying?" Amber asked, tossing the blade to her other hand and backing up slightly. Her hackles rose, and she ducked just in time as a spray of high-velocity darts shot over her, in the exact position her head used to be. She stole a glance behind her to see Frost standing in the middle of the entrance of a hidden door.

"So glad you could join the party," she said, smirking. If they wanted a two-on-one fight, then that's exactly what they'd get.

Amber focused on protecting herself from harm as Frost fired more darts at her. She wove between them, ducking each one. Although he continued firing at her, there was a light in his eye and a half-smile on his lips. She couldn't tell if he was deranged or actually enjoying this fight.

She picked up a geode with purple crystals exposed and tossed it over her shoulder in the direction she thought Frost was standing. She didn't wait to see if it hit him or not as she charged towards Guinevere again.

Guinevere delivered a powerful axe kick straight at her jaw.

Amber weaved to the left, dodging the blow. Stepping forward with her left leg, she jabbed upwards, hitting Guinevere squarely in the chest. While Guinevere stumbled backwards, Amber slammed her elbow into the wound at Guinevere's hip.

Blood gushed out, and Guinevere screamed, clutching one hand to her wound.

Not forgetting Frost, Amber swung around and threw the dagger. This time, she watched it sink into his abdomen. His skin paled as he attempted to withdraw the blade.

Amber swung her left leg over, twisting as she jumped in the air and performed a butterfly kick to Guinevere's chest. Her stabilizers whirred beneath her skin as she struck her opponent in the jaw. She landed on her feet and ducked as Frost wrenched the dagger from his gut and threw it at her.

The blade lodged itself in Guinevere's chest.

Amber blinked in surprise as blood bubbled on the luck-driver's lips. She coughed, trying to say something as her lungs filled with her own blood and she began to suffocate.

Amber looked back at Frost, who stood completely still, his hands shaking. Blood freely flowed from the wound on his abdomen. The tension slowly left her shoulders as she reached back and ripped the blade free from Guinevere's chest. Wiping the blood and gore from the blade on the bed sheets, Amber turned to face Frost.

His lips trembled as he watched Guinevere die. He didn't say anything to her to provide comfort. He just stood there, watching.

"Why did you save me from the woman in the tunnels?" Amber asked. Her voice was hoarse and raw. She realized that she had been screaming during the fight without even realizing it. She'd been so focused on surviving that all she could remember doing was using her abilities to manipulate where her blows landed and to avoid being struck by her opponents.

Her stabilizers continued to hum beneath her skin as she approached Frost. His cybernetic eye dimmed as he met her gaze and gave her a lopsided smile.

"I knew you were the luckiest woman on Thoth," he said.

She placed a hand on her hip and stared at him. "Tell me why you saved me in the tunnels," she commanded. She didn't have time for him to meander through random stories. She needed to know the truth.

He shrugged. "From the moment I met you, I just felt like I needed to protect you," he said.

"But why?" she pressed, unsatisfied with his response.

He sank to his knees, his hands pressing against the wound. "I'm not sure why," he admitted.

For some reason, Amber believed him. A part of her felt pity for him as he lay on the floor, bleeding out. She wasn't going to save him. He'd helped Guinevere kill Morta. He'd lied to her. Sure, he'd saved her life, but he couldn't even explain to her why he'd done it. For all she knew, it was the remnants of her power that had nudged him to save her in the tunnels beneath the city.

"I want you to know, when I leave this room, I will never think of you again," she said. "You are nothing to me, other than the person who helped kill the one person in this world who always had my back."

She glanced over her shoulder towards Guinevere. Her lifeless eyes stared at the ceiling. She couldn't tell if she was happy she hadn't been the one to deliver the death blow or not. Part of her wished it had been by her hand.

"I know," Frost said, his cybernetic eye glowed as ice began to pack into his wound, staunching the flow of blood. "But I'm not going to let myself die here."

Amber stared at him numbly. She could kill him. The whir of her stabilizers told her that she could manipulate everything about the battle such that she would always be the victor. She didn't doubt herself the way she had before. She'd manipulated the odds and beaten another luck-driver. She'd pushed her powers beyond her known boundaries to save Morta when she'd been attacked by Laurie.

With time, she could become stronger. She would build a world where nothing could harm her. Not now.

Not ever again.

189

She smiled at Frost. She wouldn't save him, but she also wouldn't manipulate the odds against him. Let the universe decide his fate.

She didn't say anything to him as she slid the dagger back into her boot and retrieved her pulser pistol from the floor. She didn't look at him as she slipped from the room as if she had never been there at all.

Her mind wandered as she stalked from the casino. She didn't see a single person as she exited the way she'd come. Thoughts of her time spent with Morta filled her mind, leaving her with a sense of wanting and sorrow.

The ache in her chest wouldn't subside, even as she began running. Towards or away from the fight, she wasn't sure. She just let the world dissolve into a blur of color and sound as she sped past buildings and down dark alleyways. Her heart hammered in her ears, slowly blocking out all other sound. Her chest burned, dimming the emotional ache.

Her calves began to tremble as she raced up a hill. Higher and higher she climbed until she at last crested its top and looked back at the city. Neon lights highlighted darker buildings. Scantily clad women danced on rooftops. The sounds of drinking and fighting filled the ever-twilight horizon.

She smiled as she stared out at the 'V.'

She was the queen of the Underworld now.

This was all hers.

The End...

The Fortuna Saga Continues in Suicide King

More Books by S.A. McClure

The Fortuna Saga

Suicide King (coming soon)

Dead Man's Hand (coming soon)

All or Nothing (coming soon)

The Valka Chronicles

Spellbreaker

Starseeker

Dreamwalker (coming soon)

Broken Prophecies Series

Kilian: A Broken Prophecies Story

Keepers of the Light

Destroyers of the Light

Harbinger of the Light

Apprentice's Wings

Wings of Gold & Snow

Wings of Shadow & Wrath (coming soon)

Wings of Steel & Valor (coming soon)

About the Author

S.A. McClure is an avid lover of all things fantasy and science-fiction. A self-proclaimed nerd, S.A. enjoys attending comic cons, seeing new movies, and discussing books with friends. By day, she spends her time working with college students and by night she writes. When S.A. McClure isn't traveling, she's at home, wrangling her three trouble-making cats.

Read More from S.A. McClure

https://www.samcclure.com/

Connect with S.A. McClure

Instagram: sa_mcclure

Twitter: sa_mcclure

Facebook: SAMcClureLunameed